Chick Lit

On the Edge:
New Womens Fiction Anthology

Chick-Lit

On the Edge:
New Womens Fiction Anthology

Edited by
Cris Mazza
Jeffrey DeShell

Published by FC2 with support given by the English
Department Unit for Contemporary Literature of
Illinois State University and the Illinois Arts
Council

Address all inquiries to: FC2, Unit for Contemporary
Literature, Campus Box 4241, Illinois State University, Normal, IL 61790-4241

Chick-Lit
Cris Mazza

ISBN: Paper: 1-57366-005-1, $11.95

Produced and printed in the United States of America

Cover art: Andi Olsen
Cover design: Don Bergh
Book design: David Dean

The editors wish to acknowledge and thank the following for their assistance with and enthusiasm for this project:

Michael Anania
Jennifer Skaja
Keeli Ellison
John Lowney
Ashley J. Cross
Susan Mikula

Contents

Introductions

Jan Nystrom — *The Young Lady Who Fell From A Star* 12

Vicki Lindner — *Mother is Dying* 20

Kim Addonizio — *Reading* 32

Suzanne Greathouse — *Operator Seven* 36

Carole Maso — *Sappho Sings The World Ecstatic* 42

Kat Meads — *In The Guise Of An Explanation Of My Aunt's Life* 52

Elisabeth Sheffield — *Sugar Smacks* 58

Diane Goodman — *Crimes* 72

Laurie Foos — *Rescue Fantasies* 76

Peggy Shinner — *Our Bodies Spoke In Tongues* 84

Lily James — *Up There* 90

Thalia Field — *A ∴ I* 102

mary hope whitehead lee — *story* 120

Lisa Natalie Pearson — *Stage Fright* 126

Laura Mullen — *His Father* 142

Nicolette De Csipkay — *The Cat Lady* 146

Jonis Agee — *Mustard* 152

Lara Anderson Love — *Skittles* 160

Judith Johnson — *Asylum* 170

Carolyn Banks — *Random Violence* 182

Stacey Levine — *Scoo Boy* 190

Eileen A. Joy — *Lot's Wife* 196

What Is Postfeminist Fiction?

When the call-for-manuscripts for *On the Edge: New Women's Fiction Anthology* went out in June 1994, I asked for postfeminist writers working with alternative fiction. I just thought "postfeminist" was a funky word—possibly a controversial one if read "*anti* feminist"—so I didn't define it. I probably couldn't have if I wanted to. It was almost a joke, an ice-breaker. I just wanted to see what it would produce. I knew I was looking for something different, something that stretched the boundaries of what has been considered "women's writing," something that might simply be called "*writing*" without defining it by gender, and yet at the same time speak the diversity and depth of what women writers *can* produce rather than what they're expected to produce. The result is here within these pages. I found that articulating what *is* the different sort of fiction I was seeking to include was best accomplished by looking afterwards at the pieces assembled between the covers. And, naturally, it was actually the combining of the 400 manuscripts answering the original call for "postfeminist writing" with the perception of the editors selecting the eventual contents of the book that produced an answer—at least our answer—to the question on the flier: *"What is Postfeminist fiction?"*

Not anti-feminist at all, but also ***not:*** my body, myself
my lover left me and I am so sad
all my problems are caused by men
... but watch me roar
what's happened to me is deadly
serious
SOCIETY HAS GIVEN ME AN EATING DISORDER
a poor self esteem,
a victim's perpetual fear
... therefore I'm not responsible for my
actions

With titles like *Scoo Boy, Skittles, Mustard, Sugar Smacks,* and *The Young Lady Who Fell From a Star,* I can tell these women are grinning (or sneering) as they write. Their fiction takes an often irreverent slant on the very issues women *are* concerned about, their styles and forms are at times quirky, droll, jocular, frisky, ironic, but still their fictions carry weight and power. And what do they write *about?* People who make life decisions by playing board games, male impotence therapy groups run by women counselors, an obese woman paying nickels and quarters for attention from teenage girls, a deranged hair stylist and her disloyal dog, a surreal landscape constantly producing the body of a woman's mother, a TV drama happening in *front* of the neighbor's television screen. Yet none of these are comedy, none written for laughs alone, the point *not,* in self defense, to turn laughter *at* a women's concerns into laughter *with* a woman. The trash of life *can* be funny, especially when, as writers, *we're* the ones in control. But irreverence is not mere dismissal nor a designation of insignificance. Maybe women are simply no longer afraid to honestly assess and define themselves without having to live up to standards imposed by either a persistent patriarchal world or the insistence that we achieve self-empowerment.

I realized there *is* such a thing as postfeminist writing. It's writing that says women are independent & confident, but not lacking in their share of human weakness & not necessarily self-empowered; that they are dealing with who they've made themselves into rather than blaming the rest of the world; that women can use and abuse another human being as well as anyone; that women can be conflicted about what they want and therefore get nothing; that women can love until they hurt someone, turn their own hurt into love, refuse to love, or even ignore the notion of love completely as they confront the other 90% of life. Postfeminist writing says we don't have to be superhuman anymore. Just human.

Cris Mazza

Over The Edge: On Being A Male Editor of A Woman's Anthology
An Introduction of Sorts

You want to know what happened. Exactly what happened. I don't know what I would do without you.

This takes place just inside the city, where he stayed. A place on the map, a motel for fossils that slip out at night and skulk along the cooled sidewalks, leaning back flat against painted wood, familiar patterns of bones casting Sanskrit shadows. The building is something like a castle, something like a factory, something like a warehouse, something like a prison. The apartment is small, sparse. A lacquered pine coffee table, slick, unscratched. Books everywhere: piled on the nightstand, floating on the rumpled covers, lined up on brick and board shelves and on the windowsill.

She suggested they play a game. "There— can you feel it kicking? Feel it again. Can you feel it in there?" The silence becomes louder.

His nose and dick are both hard, and Paul is on the roof on top of the skylight looking down. He's about forty-five. He is a nervous sort of animal, always sniffing and poking around. He plays golf and dresses in the latest fashions. The horrors of bad metal.

Her age and face are covered in soft blue printed cotton. These bruises are there, still, twelve days after "the incident." Though she was weary of life, she was not ready to have it end so suddenly.

Love talk? Sex talk? What does he want? Why is his behavior so inconsistent? Some say it's the glasses? Others the hair? If she was any kind of expert, she should come up with something, don't you think?

She never gets what she wants. Delicacy.

She left this morning, letting the door slam behind her. She did not say when she would be back. They fought because he forgot to buy bread.

"I hate daddy," she says, and then laughs wildly. Without a body it seem. This is not an imagined life but a lived one.

He hates to cry. He wants her. Her lovely mouth. Her throat. What's it mean when safety like that disappears from the world? His face is thick with grief. "I was always the one left out." But every thing has its up side, right?

Jeffrey DeShell

Jan Nystrom

The Young Lady Who Fell From A Star

Jan Nystrom has an MFA in creative writing from the
University of Utah and has published fiction in several
literary magazines including *North American Review, Carolina Quarterly, Indiana Review,* and *Prairie Schooner.* She
has finished her first collection of stories titled *Women
Who Fly* and is working on a magical-realistic novel set in
Southern Utah about ravens, coyotes, and wooden Indians.

The Young Lady Who Fell From A Star

1

Before *The Wizard of Oz* is released to the public, it is given a private showing. Small children attending the screening run from the room in terror. MGM goes back to work. They cut the most menacing lines from the mouth of the Wicked Witch of the West. The Witch is now just an angry old woman, a crazy old woman living in her castle on the hill.

2

There are three Totos used in the filming of *The Wizard of Oz*. Two Totos are alive and identical, so identical even the experts no longer know which Toto is which. Which Toto escapes from Mira Gulch. Which Toto runs down the yellow brick road. Which Toto likes to chase cats and which Toto risks his life for Dorothy. Of course both Totos would do that. Both Totos adore Dorothy. Both Totos would run back to the witch's castle with or without Tin Man and Scarecrow and Lion.

The third Toto isn't a real Toto at all, but a stuffed animal lying perfectly still in the field of red poppies.

3

The flashiest of all the munchkins is a little man named Billy Curtis. He smokes cigarettes. He drives to work in a full-sized car. He tells stories in which he is the hero. When Margaret Hamilton shakes her broom and bursts into flames, he is the one to extinguish her. When Judy Garland falls in love with David Rose, he helps her escape MGM and takes her to the skating rink where night after night she meets her lover. But

Margaret Hamilton does not remember any heroic munchkins and Judy Garland does not remember Billy Curtis.

After the filming of *The Wizard of Oz*, most of the munchkins disappear into the midwest. But Billy Curtis lives in Hollywood and marries two full-sized women. When he is an old man, he says that life has taught him two things: small people are clannish and big people are liars and cheats.

4

The lion is Zeke. The Scarecrow is Hunk. The Tin Man is Hickory. The Wizard is Professor Marvel. Toto is Toto. That's the magic of being a dog. The Wicked Witch of the West is Mira Gulch. But who is Glinda the Good Witch of the North?

5

When Dorothy falls to the Land of Oz, Glinda introduces her by singing to the munchkins: *Come out, come out, wherever you are and meet the young lady who fell from a star. She fell from the sky, she fell very far, and Kansas she says is the name of her star. She brings you good news or haven't you heard? When she fell from the sky, a miracle occurred.*

But Dorothy doesn't care about miracles and witch hunts; she doesn't mean to land her house on the Wicked Witch of the East anymore than she means to melt the Wicked Witch of the West with a pail of soapy water. Dorothy wants only the familiar, Kansas and the click click click of her heels on the slatted wooden porch of Auntie Em's house.

6

One munchkin named Olive falls in love with Scarecrow. She wants to be the woman to catch Scarecrow in her arms when he falls from his post. If she were Dorothy, she would lie down in the field of corn to cushion his fall.

7

When Dorothy looks out the window she sees trees, chickens, roosters on a barn roof, an old woman knitting in a rocking chair, two men in a rowboat (at this point, Toto hides under the bed), and Mira Gulch who turns into a witch in mid-air.

8

Frank Baum, the author of *The Wizard of Oz*, is born in Chittenango, New York in 1856 to a wealthy oil family. He moves to the then-frontier of South Dakota and runs a general store. When biographers write about Baum, they make him into a hero: kind, charitable, full of a sense of wonder. When he has money, Baum and his wife Maud live in Hollywood in a house they call Ozcot. In Ozcot, Baum grows prize dahlias and chrysanthemums and wins twenty-one cups in a flower show. He plays golf and dresses in the latest fashions.

9

Things that are red: Glinda's lips, the field of poisonous poppies, the bow in Lion's hair, Tin Man's heart, the sand in the Witch's hourglass, Dorothy's ruby slippers.

10

In real life, the Munchkins are awful little people. Nobody likes them. Not even Dorothy. They range in size from 2'3" to 4'8". Most of the munchkins are hypopituitary dwarfs—men and women who will never reach full size, but remain tiny, perfectly formed, sexually undeveloped. Most of the men will never grow beards. In the morning, the munchkins drink coffee from children's tea sets. They call everyone over five feet high a big person. They dislike children.

At night, they turn Culver City upside down. They roll into tight knots like bread dough on the floor of their hotel rooms. The big people say their sexual appetites are out of proportion to their size.

In the early morning hours, the policemen sweep the streets of Culver City and carry the munchkins home in huge butterfly nets.

11

Toto doesn't care much about getting back to Kansas: the predictable gray sky and nothing to do all day but chase Mira Gulch's cat. Toto knows better than to worry about Auntie Em. Auntie Em will be standing in her kitchen battering chicken thighs. She will forget Dorothy.

Besides, Toto is happy in Oz. He likes the munchkins. They make him feel serious and important. He is a favorite of the flying monkeys. He is best friends with Lion. More and more often he thinks of himself as a brave and clever dog. But when Dorothy clutches him in her arms and clicks her heels, Toto looks at Dorothy with adoring eyes and he knows his fate is sealed. He thinks, "There's no place like home. There's no place like home. There's no place like home."

12

The director of *The Wizard of Oz* is Victor Fleming. Like Toto, Victor does not like cats. When the cats howl in the hills above his Bell Air home, he shoots them and lines their bodies up outside his bedroom door. Once, angry at his wife for having brought her marmoset monkey to a restaurant, he kills a fly, mashes it, sprinkles it with salt and pepper and eats it.

13

SEVEN FACTS:

Judy Garland's real name is Frances Gumm. She used to sing with her sisters Mary Jane and Virginia. Together, they were the Singing Gumm Sisters.

Before Judy Garland can play Dorothy, MGM has to fix her teeth. Her teeth look like the white picket fence around Auntie Em and Uncle Henry's farm.

Ray Bolger is supposed to play the role of the Tin Man, but he refuses. He says, "I'm not a tin performer. I'm a fluid performer."

The horses of a different color are painted with Jell-O. This makes things difficult because the horses lick each other colorless between shots.

The billowy sky of Oz is the inside of a six foot fish tank.

The tornado is a muslin wind sock.

Toto is afraid of horses.

14

MGM shoots lots of footage of Toto escaping from the haunted castle, but Toto is so cute that everyone fears he has become the star of the film. Judy Garland is being overshadowed by her dog. MGM goes back to work. They cut scene after scene of Toto running down the castle steps and through the haunted forest.

15

The Wicked Witch of the West is beautifully wicked. She never gets what she wants. It is the only role for an ugly woman to play.

16

Judy Garland is a dancer and that is why David Rose wants her on the nights she escapes from MGM and twirls around the skating rink. He watches. Her skirt flies up. Her hair flies down. Her arms fly out. He wants her. MGM wants her.

17

For Professor Marvel's coat, the wardrobe man, Victor Fleming and Frank Morgan go to a second-hand store and chose a Prince Albert coat with a black broadcloth and a velvet collar. They want faded elegance. One afternoon, Professor Marvel turns his pocket inside out and reads, "L. Frank Baum."
This is a true story. Frank and Victor and Professor Marvel swear on it.

18

Less than a month before the filming of *The Wizard of Oz* is over and Margaret Hamilton is having dinner with a friend. She is feeling generous and relieved. She is tired of acting with monkeys. She insists on paying for dinner, but when she reaches for her purse, she leans into the candlelight and her friend says, "Margaret do you feel all right?" Margaret's skin has turned green from the copper pigment in the witch paint.

19

Desire is a foolish thing, but only Toto understands this. Dorothy wants to get back to Kansas where one day is just like the next and the landscape is as flat and bland as a pancake. The Tin Man wants a heart so he can be jealous and devoted. The

Scarecrow wants a brain so he can tell people why the ocean meets the shore. The Wicked Witch of the West wants to make Tin Man into a beehive and Scarecrow into a mattress. Only Lion has any sense: he wants to be King of the Forest.

Off camera, Toto and Lion are best friends. Lion says things like, "What makes the muskrat guard his musk? Courage." And Toto puffs out his chest and struts around the empty set. Normally a pusillanimous dog, he practices bravery and Lion applauds. When Dorothy is trapped by the Wicked Witch of the West, Toto is the first one to go back to save her. But that is not bravery. That is love. Even Toto does not escape desire.

20

The Wicked Witch of the West goes on to make Folger's coffee commercials.

Toto, the favorite dog of his trainer Spitz, retires and eats roast beef from silver platters.

Scarecrow, Lion, and Tin Man go on to have undistinguished careers.

Dorothy kills herself.

The Munchkins disappear by busloads into the midwest and are never seen again.

21

In the book *The Wizard of Oz*, when Dorothy leaves Oz, she rolls out of the sky and tumbles onto the prairies of Kansas. Uncle Henry is milking cows. Auntie Em is watering cabbages. Toto begins to bark and Dorothy says, "Hello Auntie Em. I've been to the land of Oz, but I'm so glad I'm home."

In the Hollywood version it is all illusion. Nothing has changed. After the tornado, after the credits roll up the screen, Mira Gulch comes back. She wants Toto. This time, she twists the lid of her basket shut with a piece of bailing twine. Toto will never get away.

22

Dorothy makes it back to Kansas: past the friendly little men in their green felt hats; past the monkeys who would tear her limb to limb; past Tin Man, Lion, and Scarecrow: the men who would make her their princess; and, with the help of Toto, she makes it past the Wizard, the man who would feed her crumbs from the palm of his hand and tell her he is magic until she believes him, until she begins to hunger, until, floating above Oz in his colored balloon, she begins to starve.

Vicki Lindner

Mother Is Dying

Vicki Lindner is an essayist, journalist, and fiction writer. Her pieces have recently appeared in *New York Woman, Ploughshares, The Kenyon Review, The Little Magazine, Fiction, Frontiers, Northern Lights,* and *The South Dakota Review.* She teaches writing at the University of Wyoming.

Mother is Dying

The night Mother died I dreamed I was a man. Mother didn't actually die that night—she cried out in her sleep and fell into a coma. And what I dreamed was that I was sexually molested on a desiccated flood plain by a slim, red-haired woman. When she unzipped her black jeans, pendulous hairy balls spilled out of the placket. Later, as the plane leaving Cheyenne bucked into cold gusts, I realized that the androgyne looked just like me, the same dry hennaed curls and stained cashmere sweater.

I had visited Mother a few weeks before. At that time her feet were swollen. She pulled off her red wool socks and showed me her toes, curved by tight shoes into bloated tubers. CYTOXIN, TAMOXIFEN, MEXALTIL, NOVALDEX, CARDIZEM and LANOXIN were spread out before her on the formica table. COMPOSINE allowed her to eat. Brown junkets picked grains of millet from the feeder outside the kitchen window and warbled them back. "I had a bad night," she announced in tones indicating it was her duty to impart undesirable facts. Downstairs in the basement, reeking of mould, I saw that her prized primrose seedlings, sprouting infantile leaves, were dry, almost crisp. I then understood that she could no longer walk down the stairs to water them, to the scene of her life—the old washing machine, the cans of tomatoes, soup and safflower oil, stored in the garage with fertilizer. Upstairs the yellow place mats remained unlaundered. But in the cardboard room that used to be mine, slowly bending and straightening, dying fingers ungnarling themselves around sheets, she made up the bed beneath a photo of my self—a seventeen-year-old frowning virgin, milking a cow at the country fair. After this innocent picture was taken I defied her with a black track star in the New Jersey swamps.

The poodles ran barking wild tenors to the doorbell. They were louder now, dominated the house. Outside traffic coursed around the two million dollar fake colonials that had obliterated toadstools in once vacant lots. Mother sat on the couch while I read *Mr. Palomar*. She always talked while I read. "When you were a little girl you used to cry, 'You love Roger more than you do me,'" she confided yet again and chuckled, bemused, as she always does when she repeats this, to imply we both know how untrue it was. I thought, "I'm not a fool now and I wasn't then," and turned my eyes back to the book angrily, although I knew she was dying and we had made our peace. Then she uttered a sentence, altogether new:

"Your father's mother was a tartar!" she said.

When she was taking a shower Dad asked, "Ahem...How does Mother seem?" For a millisecond he looked baffled:

"I thought her heart was all right..."

She had told me that he suggested she swim laps, ride her exercycle, choke down vitamins, while ADRIAMYCIN scoured her veins.

"Are you crazy?" she asked him.

That night she felt too sick to eat. Dad and I sat at the table alone. "Ahem...Did you know that Jerusalem was once the center of the Christian World?" he inquired. He listened, but did not hear, as I spoke, my tongue maneuvering through blockades of fragmented words.

When I was washing dishes Mother regained strength; she reoccupied the kitchen:

"You're using the *dog's* sponge, for God's sake!"

"Don't put that bowl in the bottom of the dishwasher!" she cried, the burden of irritation in her voice familiar, yet startling, the wail of a smoke alarm when there is no fire. Then she turned viciously on Dad for sticking the rising bread dough in the fridge. I watched her expand in size until she became as gargantuan as King Kong when he batted planes from the top of the skyscraper. Shrinking, I scurried away from the gorilla's roar.

On the Newark-bound jet I knew Mother was dwindling

but she was still very large I conjured up my quintessential image of her: jumping out of the bathtub the last time I ran away from home. My clothes were bundled together with $14 of baby sitting money. I had planned to walk to Route 46, flag down the bus and move to New York at the age of twelve. But Mother streaked after me, stomach heavy, wet breasts flailing, chasing me naked through her garden of rocks. She shouted, "Run! Go ahead! I'll help you pack your bags!" When I returned she had thrown the clothes I'd left on my attic room's green linoleum out the window and onto the lawn. Nine years later a black man pitched and heaved in my apartment; Mother called, "Just to see if something's wrong." Eight years after that Kenzo declared, "You have a will, like Nixon!" and went back to Osaka. Mother, her hands on the succulent ocher goblets of Iris, declared, "That's what they did to our boys in the war," and said she wouldn't pretend that she wasn't glad. And when I lay, eye swollen shut, nose broken, in the Government Public Hospital in Aswan, Sister Vittoria insisted that I write Mother a postcard to assure her that I was having a good time:

"When you cried for help, your Mother, she heard you."

Mother read my scrawled message and said, "You're lucky you still have a daughter," to Dad.

But the night she died I mean went into a coma I was safely contained in a tight brown house in a university town. I was forty-three years old. I had a white man and a job.

In October she informed me the cancer was back. She had known this for awhile, wanted to spare me, starting a new job. "The liver is a vital organ," she sighed in the same tone she had used to tell me she would help pack my bags. I went to The Buckhorn Bar and beneath the stuffed moose head and two-headed calf, I cried.

At Christmas dinner Mother suddenly stopped eating. She grew pale and shrunk, green fumes curling around her pointed leather shoes. Dad lead her away. "There's no need for everyone to be involved in this," he authorized.

He cried, "Call the doctor."

Roger and I remained at the dining room table, tense, crumbling jelly snow tops, hacking at the traditional white fruit cake, stirring tea. Once again I expressed my theory that

Mother's doctors were stupid and her treatment wasn't right. Roger yelled that I was a know-it-all.

"Health-obsessed!" he stood up and shouted.

Then he referred to what I had said about his tiny round wife—that I hoped she would *deign* to come for Christmas, too. "Deign," he quoted. "I almost drove up there and punched you out for that!" His nose and mouth jutted forward like a pronghorn's snout.

"For years I tried to make you like me," he shouted. "I invited you to my wedding because I wanted you to like me. But now," his loud voice cracked, "I don't like you. We have nothing in common!" He implied that I live an unnatural existence, unmarried, isolated.

I said, "You don't know shit about my life."

About "nothing in common" I said, "That's right!"

"You think you're a big success..." he yelled.

"Instead of a failure like you?"

"I don't care!" His lean shoulders shot up to his frizzy corona in a fake indifferent shrug.

Then we slouched toward the bedroom to look at Mother. She sat on the edge of her sexless twin wearing pilled polyesters from The Salvation Army, though Dad is a millionaire. Her big head was bowed, her thickening hands pressed between her knees; her flimsy rayon turban had slipped and we could see that what was left of her hair, dyed red like mine, was being pushed away by a sparse blue fringe. Dad was reading her Christmas cards from friends; the two of them were closer than they had ever been.

"We don't all have to be involved in this," he stated.

They looked down at the cards again; they didn't look up. Roger, myself, our furious voices, even the snappish black poodles, and above all, Christmas dinner with the entire family present had been eclipsed.

Later I went into the kitchen and told my brother that I had always liked him. The middle-aged man was washing dishes and appeared to be sobbing.

Seven hours after leaving Cheyenne I waited in the green hospital with Roger and Dad. We forced ourselves to look at Mother in the coma. For all practical purposes, she was gone.

24

Her open eyes stared, her lips twitched back from her teeth. Her elbows, wired to monitors, bent like the stripped wooden joints of a tinker toy. Her evaporating skin, stretched over her bones, shone like a pearlized shell vacated by oyster. Her breath, squeezed in and out of her body by a grunting machine, was bad. Roger, her favorite, couldn't take it. He went back to the suburban house, a pack of cards, and began to sort her recipe collection—yeasted waffles, chicken Lombreglia, fish Florentine. He made and froze stews for the future of Dad. He baked Mother's repertoire of cakes: moist Orange Sponge, the timeless Triple Chocolate, Mocha with Rum Flavored Cream. He threw her pills in the trash.

I stayed at the hospital. Dad was trying to convince the young doctor to unplug Mother. "AHEM...Hal...May I call you Hal?...You didn't know my wife...She was vital, active..."

"She made fifteen jars of mixed citrus marmalade the day before..." I had been about to say, "the day before she died...."

Dad continued, "She was the last person who would have wanted to live like...this. She had a living will. I can show it to you." His hands groped, wet, sticky starfish, for the young doctor's arm. Then he cried, a shocking sound, like a carp roaring.

A day later Mother began to thrash. At first I had felt that she knew I was in the room with her; I intuited her familiar forbearance of her peculiar single daughter, the fury that sparked our mutual acknowledgement about to burn the hospital down. Not anymore. Her arms and legs beat at Gorgons parading through her Bardo. Life was a plexiglass capsule her hard, syncopated limbs were beating to crack.

"Like a chicken with its head cut off!" wept Dad.

He couldn't stand it; he begged the doctors to unplug her. He went into her room alone, hovered over her escaping body, and howled:

"MARY, MARY"

I had heard it was important to say goodbye. Tomorrow I had to fly west to the university town. I touched Mother's huge hand—the thinning gold band stuck beneath the swollen knuckle, the fungus, caught from wet, fecund soil, collected beneath her broken ridged nails. I like to think that after ten months with the shrink I had made my peace. "Goodbye, Mother," I said and felt absurd. You can't say goodbye to your DNA, your inured *michigas*, the inspiration for the iconoclasm you have spent your life waving like an enemy flag.

Then I returned to the house of cards. I invaded her boudoir, repository for twin beds shared with the dogs. Her thin brown glasses lay on the scratched dresser's mahogany veneer where she put them to rest before she died I mean went into a coma. The specs were lifeless without the animating glint of her resigned lashless eyes. I opened the drawer and scrabbled down through layers of soap and shampoo samples to the diaries she kept during World War II after she married Dad. I didn't have to read them again; I knew what they said:

There wasn't always time to make love.

They fought because he forgot to buy bread.

They both cherished colds.

She would never save enough money to buy all the things she wanted, so she might as well go ahead and have a child.

Dad had already given me her jewelry, stashed in the basement in a detergent box. There was a string of creamy round pearls, a wedgewood and silver bracelet, a Florentine ring, the thick gold hoops that dragged down her earlobes. Now, I also took what I had given her back—Redwing hiking shoes, the second-hand kimono with an unfocused willow pattern I'd brought from Japan. I undid the silk chiffon scarf from the satin pocket of her grey Persian lamb. I stuffed all of it, including the jewels, into my duffel bag and flew back to the snow-covered prairie to teach *Mr. Palomar* to my advanced class.

The doctor did unplug Mother, but she continued to breathe. In the university town it snowed for forty-eight hours. The temperature dropped to thirty below. The telephone wires roared with Dad's weeping. To begin every conversation he cleared his throat:

"Ahem, the situation with Mother is this...."

The doctors refused to stop feeding her with tubes although chances were one in a million she would come out of the coma. Dad said he thought she squeezed his finger; perhaps she followed him with her eyes. Roger shouted that Mother should be allowed to Die with Dignity! Then Dad walked into the hospital room and she said Hello. He asked her to speak louder because her voice, unused in the Bardo, had become a delicate rasp. According to him she sat up and bellowed, "Is that loud enough?"

We laughed, guffawed, gasped, choked on our giggles. Roger said, "Are you sitting down? Are you ready for this?" Our Mother, as invincible as King Kong in the jungle, had vanquished death. But this was false pride. The doctors warned that if we took her home:

Her kidneys would fail.

Without chemotherapy the cancer would get her.

She might have another heart attack, and,

of course, her brain had lost cells.

She didn't talk right; she didn't remember.

I didn't go back East on spring break. I didn't want to encounter Mother's thin phantom. I told my face in the mirror that I needed a vacation from Teaching and Death. I had said goodbye, I insisted.

We had made our Peace.

Instead the white man and I traveled through the self-absorbed Rocky mountains along the White Knuckle Highway to the frozen Tetons, down Red Canyon Pass. We fought in a Pinedale motel. Every night I called New Jersey from phone booths buffeted by dry gusts. In one outside Rawlins, Roger put Mother on the line with me.

"It's your Daughter!" he shouted to her.

I could feel her flickering intelligence activating the wires.

"I miss you," I said, although Mother was alive.

"I love you,"I said; I had never told her that before and was not sure even now that I did.

Her voice drifted through galaxies. "When will I see you?" it asked feebly but distinctly.

I flew back to New Jersey then, frantic, guilty, afraid by the time I got there Mother would be dead. On the way to the airport, five pick-ups, I counted them, had flipped and lay, wheels up, on black ice. Leaving Cheyenne, the tail of the plane shook.

Ten hours later I am feeding Mother soup. Vases bursting with April daffodils lure her eyes to their former delight. She is as small, thin and mighty as Mahatma Ghandi. Her bones have sucked water from her camellia-colored skin. Her eyes are no longer blue but the hue of the shadow clouds in a blue sky cast. Mother is beautiful, I am amazed to think. It is difficult to spoon liquid down the throat of her prone rubbery body. Her stomach is distended. I know she wears a diaper though I do not look. I am glad I can say I think we have made our peace before this. Her lips pull back:

"Uhhhh huhhhhhh," she sighs and intakes her breath.

In the undersized cardboard bed, I dream I am semiconscious in the back of a rattletrap car; Mother is driving me through a canyon of red sandstone, straight to the heart of a burned, toppled city that lies blurred beneath smoke.

Dad leans over Mother's pillow with shocked, affectionate eyes. He calls her "Honey," as he might a small, helpless child. "One, two..." His fingers wave in front of her face as he helps her relearn to count.

She reaches into an empty river to rescue the drowned numbers. "Tell-me-what-I-am-missing," she recites. She sees him, but his face is not in her eyes.

I balance the glass of red juice on her chest, thread the straw between her dry lips. Our conversation runs counterpoint to a cosmic humming, a drumming in the spheres:

AUM.

"Dad is in the kitchen having dinner," I provide. Actually he is drinking peach schnapps with the black weekday nurse, a former dancer, who no one can believe is sixty- five.

Mother blows thin, watery bubbles. "Daddy is having dinner with Kyle?" Kyle is her youngest brother who died in the saddle. Her father has been dead time out of mind.

Next winter my father and I will walk through frozen goldenrod with the noisy poodles. The old one will be blinded by cataracts then. You do not know all the details of Mother's death, he will tell me, how she felt, what she said. You do not know what the nurse did to her...

"Going...going...gone," the black nurse summarizes.

I dream about the track star I defied her with. He is

running down Grand Street, dark legs flashing beneath red silk trunks.

I look for him in the grey concrete whorls but find only drops of his blood.

Dad comes in while I am feeding Mother soup. Stridently he sings "Three Blind Mice." He urges Mother to join in.

"Dad! For Christ's Sake!" Roger screams over the phone.

The youthful black nurse cannot lift Mother. The two of them fall, falling, falling, slow motion to the floor and lie there for minutes, hours perhaps. Mother's eyes, unperturbed, stare up peacefully. The nurse rises like smoke, adjusts her blonde wig, and prepares to spend the weekend "fightin and cavilin with that man I've lived with for twenty-five years."

I read to Mother from *Alice in Wonderland*. Her face assumes a familiar attentive outline for a moment. I remember that she always listened alertly when I spoke. Then her fingers begin to move, threshing the bedclothes. The white rabbit disappears down the hole.

The night she really dies, and I do not know it, a pain will enter my head like an arrow as I walk on ice on an unplowed road. I will close the door on the lyrical guitar at The Pahaska Tepee, sleep and sleep.

"I live in Wyoming now," I tell Mother. Her ears are clearly devoid of the gold hoops I took.

"Wy-Om-ing?" she repeats with a convincing imitation of vacant wonderment.

Before I left for the faraway university town, we sat on the terrace, under the bird feeder. "If I outlive your father I will move closer to your brother in Albuquerque," she said in a pious voice. Worse luck for her favorite, my inner voice spoke, snide, but hurt. Then she intoned what a good son Roger was, how he called every weekend, how long they did talk.

I push an African violet onto Mother's chest, remembering this. When she said that she had known she was dying; the cancer was in her liver; she would not outlive Dad. She was delivering her final message, rubbing it in. Now, her thickened fingers, impelled by her nervous system, not desire, feel their way to a curled yellow leaf. They pluck it off, but I can see that her brain cells fail to register the death of the leaf.

I will not cry in or near the New Jersey swamps.

The new weekend nurse, an African woman, the conical shape of a rusty Nevada mountain, easily lifts Mother. "Why he in bed?" she asks rhetorically. "He get bed sores in bed. He can sit in wheelchair! He can wear his real clothes. Look all these clothes," she remonstrates, pushing hangers in the closet. 'What, you going to send his clothes to Salvation Army now?"

Burrowing through her drawers and into the closet floor where her pointy-toed shiny shoes march, we will pull stretched Orlon sweaters, dark, grainy hose, a polyethylene wig form, a big Mexican purse out of the depths. As we stuff this into cardboard boxes, I will discover a gold pin she wore in her youth on a polyester vest—a beautiful, cross-legged Chinese sage with a wise, ivory face.

We thrust daffodils, tulips and roses toward Mother's dull eyes. "Tell-me-what-I-am-missing," she murmurs.

Dad's starfish fingers grope toward the conical African nurse. "Ahem. I don't know what I would do without you." His shoulders dissolve; his eyelids shade.

I close the hollow door of my former bedroom, insert the heavy gold hoops in my ears. They catch in my dry hennaed curls and glint. I do not look, as I expected, like a Gypsy or Madame or Man in Drag. Months later I will pull one off when I remove my hat, realize it is missing, search, and find it, half-buried in a drift on my block: A miracle? A sign of what?

You need to drink. Take a little juice. Take a little tea! Are you sure you can't sip a little more water?

I dream I am in a moist greenhouse. Orchids and Birds of Paradise hang disembodied in its rain forest air. Mother appears in a wheelchair, wearing a shapeless pants suit, her brown glasses replaced. Her expression is calm, serious, concentrated. "She's back!" I think and feel the soaring joy some dreams permit. But her highlighted bones, her fringe of blue hair, signal that, no, Mother is still dead. Yet she expands in size, rises, and escorts me through her garden of rocks. Wordless, she points out clusters of mountain pinks, rare yellow primroses, bushes energetic with red azaleas. The sun falls, shooting points of light like a Fourth of July sparkler. The sky turns the color of fool's gold. A cone-shaped fluorescent lavender blossom, composed of countless florets, descends, pushing away the gilded dusk. The garden is silent. Then an armored moving van rolls into the yard and parks. A uniformed attendant opens the shiny plated door. Mother enters. The door slams shut.

The next day I have to fly back. The white man will pick me up at the airport; my duffel is packed. I said goodbye to Mother long ago, perhaps at the hour of my birth. Sitting in her metal wheelchair, she examines a tangle of oxygen molecules. Grocery coupons the nurse has given her scatter in her lap. I will carry her ashes up to Medicine Bow Peak and shake them loose over bullet-colored granite, send them flying down to the cold glacial lake, beside an uncultivated meadow of Sego lilies. But first I encourage her to drink a little water. Is there some place she would like me to roll her, I ask. She understands; her swollen finger points toward the picture window that surveys the scarred oak, stunted by lightning, the unweeded flower beds, the Crayola green lawn—the scene of her life.

"There. In the sunlight," Mother shouts.

Kim Addonizio

Reading

Kim Addonizio is the author of a collection of poems, *The Philosopher's Club* (BOA Editions). Her fiction has recently appeared in *Frighten the Horses*, *Gettysburg Review*, and in an anthology from the Crossing Press, *Breaking Up is Hard to Do*. She lives in San Francisco.

Reading

I'm sick in bed with a high fever and I'm reading. First I read in the newspaper about how dead bodies are used as crash test dummies in order to improve safety equipment in cars. Then I go to the bathroom and read the *New Yorker*, where I find out about Cambodian women who went blind after the Khmer Rouge soldiers came to their villages, tortured their neighbors and swung their kids by the heels to smash their heads open on palm tree trunks. I go back to bed, my head aching, my body burning up, and read a short story about a guy who has an affair with his sister's Barbie. The sister mutilates Barbie—eats her feet off, gives her a partial masectomy, sets her on fire. The masectomy reminds me of something in the novel I started last night. A man who unloads bricks of cellophane from boxcars all day undresses a woman who turns out to have a huge, rock-hard lump in her breast. When I fell asleep, she was sitting in the Emergency Room and he was headed for the door, feeling sick. I finish the story about Barbie—it's the last one in the book—and masturbate for a while, then wonder what to read next. A fat black animal with yellow eyes is sitting at the end of the bed, staring at me like I'm insane, like it has to watch me every minute for fear of what I'll do next. I read once that cats hate to be stared at, that they take it as a sign of aggression. What you're supposed to do, meeting a strange cat for the first time, is look at it, blink and then cut your eyes quickly away, at the carpet or something. I try this on my cat but she's suddenly disappeared. I look around the room. Books everywhere piled on the nightstand, floating on the rumpled covers, lined up on brick-and-board shelves and on the windowsill.

There's a stack of magazines in a yellow basket in the bathroom, magazines on the back of the toilet along with a book that has photos of Elvis impersonators and quotes from them about what it's like pretending to be Elvis. The next time I go to the bathroom I take some Tylenol and read in the introduction that Elvis is a bonafide American icon who lives in our collective unconscious, along with Davy Crockett, Johnny Appleseed, Wyatt Earp, and Pecos Bill. One of the impersonators, when he's not being Elvis, works as a hospital technician. I can't finish the *New Yorker* article yet; when I got to the part about the kids and the palm trees I put it down. I have to read it slowly, the way you can take belladonna in small doses so it won't kill you, just make you high and disoriented and give you hallucinations that make you think you're someplace you aren't. You might feel, for example, like you're at home in your own bed with fever when you're really dying in a hospital, blind from everything you've tried not to see. You're convinced you're someone else, and when that person dies men in coveralls take the body and strap it into a car and send it slamming into a brick wall, then extract it from the crumpled wreckage and study it, making the world a little bit safer, the product a little bit better, the whole thing that much easier to bear.

Suzanne Greathouse

Operator Seven

Suzanne Greathouse lives in Bellingham, Washington where she both practices and teaches creative and technical writing. She is currently at work on a collection of short stories and is co-authoring a creative writing textbook which examines the limited vision, often racist and sexist, of the dominant aesthetic. Her short stories and poems have appeared in a variety of journals. She has a fondness for sleazy waterfront bars and tattoos.

Operator Seven

We are all quite baffled by Operator Seven. She appeared several weeks ago, discovered by the Salon owner. She was just sitting there when he opened up—at station seven—drinking coffee and reading a magazine.

All her documents are in order, pasted above her mirror like those of every other beauty operator, but she vigorously refuses to wear the required Salon smock—and snorts most unattractively when informed of other requirements of a government subsidized salon. Equally as baffling is the muscular black dog with her.

The beast has made himself at home, finding a discarded basket in the storage room and helping himself to towels for bedding. He prefers to have his basket in the actual salon area as opposed to the waiting room, and growls viciously whenever someone makes an attempt to remove him from our already crowded work area. He is a nervous sort of animal, always sniffing and poking about. He shows particular interest in customer's handbags. Several of us have approached Operator Seven about this aggressive behavior, but she acts as though she has no ties to the dog and certainly no influence on him. At times, this appears to be true as neither seems to care for the other—they are constantly at odds—but there is *something* between them.

In general, we all get along with the dog. Operators Six and Four were nervous at first, having had bad experiences with dogs in the past, but they warmed up to the idea when asked to view the animal as both mascot and watch dog. In fact, now, they puff out their chests and invite others over to see if he chooses to fall asleep under their hair washing sink or meet them at the door with a wag and a lick. It is really only Operator Seven who seems to have a problem with the dog. Or is it the dog who has a problem with Operator Seven? It is difficult to say, for there are times the dog's behavior towards Operator Seven could be interpreted as affectionate. He once appropriated her smock to use in his basket. The smock was shredded like slaw but the way he plunged his nose into the polyester gave the impression he merely wanted to be close to her scent.

As much as we have all developed a fondness for the dog, the same is not true of Operator Seven, who, we have found out, was sent here to CUT HAIR. Operators Two and Five are incensed by "the cutter's" presence and have voiced a fear for the safety of themselves and their clients should certain groups find out about her. Operator Two added that she may have to quit the Salon as she was raised to believe long hair a gift from God and a strong part of a woman's identity. Others complained that it was improper for the owner to have let Operator Seven in without a vote, despite the additional business she might bring the salon.

This debate has become the preoccupation of Operators Two, Four and Six, with Two saying haircuts are blasphemous, Four that they are unpatriotic, and Six siding with the government's official stance of banning haircuts altogether for women unless the women work with machinery or have had their hair brutalized by a family member or stranger in such a way that cosmetic reparations are required. Since my job consists mostly of doing manicures and fancy braiding, I was never trained to cut hair, I don't feel it my place to voice an opinion. However, many of my clients complain about headaches related to having excessively long hair and also complain that they are housebound, given the amount of time it takes to coif. If any of the operators favor haircuts, they are afraid to step forward. The proof of this being the vote during the redesign of the Salon's *Yellow Pages* ad. A five vote majority kept the mention of hair cuts out of the advertisement—listing it simply as *And More*.

Most everyone is rude to Operator Seven, excluding her from their discussions of new techniques for coloring hair or whether a spiral perm is better than a regular perm. This chasm has been widened by Operator Seven's threatening of the dog with a hair brush and foul language after the smock incident. The dog responded to the threats by leaving a runny bowel movement in front of Operator Seven's hairdressing chair. Operators Three through Six rallied around this retaliation and have publicly joined the dog in disliking Operator Seven—they shun her at every opportunity, forgetting the fact that they *too* were trained to cut hair.

Operator Seven doesn't seem to mind being ostracized, in fact she has the calm resignation of someone used to being treated in this very way. Most days she seems oblivious to all the turmoil and discussion surrounding her presence. She carefully studies hair cutting textbooks and practices on miniature fashion dolls.

There are those occasional days when Operator Seven paces angrily in front of her station swearing about the latest anti-hair cutting demonstration or bills submitted to the government, but as a rule she keeps to herself and is most congenial when spoken too. She has even honored our request to park her automobile away from the Salon. It has a bumper sticker that says "Take a Short Cut to Autonomy."

Actually, Operator Seven has had a few clients since she arrived. The first one entered from the rear of the Salon and wore dark glasses. Her procedure took several hours and I was amazed afterwards at the amount of hair on the floor. Operators Three and Six said the sight of it made them physically ill and that they never would have stood for such a massacre except the owner had confided that this woman had been violated by an ex-boyfriend.

Before, during and after the appointment, Operator Seven was her reserved self. The dog, on the other hand, seemed to be strangely excited by this customer, barking loudly and gamboling about as though he were a pup—drawing quite a lot of attention to the scene. Once the woman left, he became sullen and refused offerings of sliced meats.

The next woman to see Operator Seven walked boldly in without an appointment, her red hair somewhat tangled and wild but very shiny and healthy. Operator Seven spent hours with this woman. We could hear their voices rising and falling like breakers.

During this haircut, the dog dragged his basket to a spot in front of the hairdressing chair and began licking himself—loudly and sloppily. The sounds were such that a person just *had* to look. Several of us thought this behavior disgusting and it had the effect of lowering our opinion of the beast—who, by the way, repeated this routine whenever a customer like the redheaded woman came in for a cut.

Operator Seven took to keeping a squirt bottle of ammonia at her station for these occasions and sprayed liberal amounts towards the dog's privates. This seemed to terminate the activity but only briefly, for the dog is of a persistent nature and has invented new ways of expressing his displeasure over Operator Seven's enthusiasm with certain clients.

More and more women started calling the Salon for haircuts after Operator Seven came on board. Many of them made appointments for other services, so we have all benefited. We were unsure if this increase in business was because of Operator Seven or because some celebrities recently went public about their own haircuts.

The increase in business has caused the dog to become even more impossible. It seems he started dialing up Operator Seven at home after hours. No one knows how he got her number because it is unpublished and not kept at the salon. Operator Seven said she was positive her caller was the dog because she recognized the slurping sounds from the salon. She has called the telephone company about this matter but they refuse to look into it. The night time disturbances have caused her to be blurry-eyed and rumpled at work?

The harassment of Operator Seven escalated beyond the phone calls. The dog began terrorizing her lunches—a bite out of a sandwich here, a bag of chips stolen there. Operator Four said she observed the dog nosing around in the refrigerator. And when pressed, Operator Two confessed to helping the beast with a ziplock bag. Operator Seven responded by putting hot pepper on Operator Two's sandwich. She sat in her chair all afternoon, snipping the air with her shears, waiting to see the results.

Despite our tentative acceptance of Operator Seven, she still makes us anxious. She does not seem to be taking the harassment very well. She is sometimes listless and untidy, not a good advertisement for the salon, making it difficult to treat her as part of the team.

We are confused, as well, about how to behave around the dog. Half the operators feel *he* is not the problem. The day five protesters started pursuing Operator Seven up the walk, the dog seemed almost sympathetic, growling and lunging at the troublemakers to drive them off. Still, he has not given up his antics. He caused Operator Seven to trip, fall and sprain her wrist during the fracas. She was unable to work for days. The dog brought her aspirin every four hours, kept watch at the Salon door, but appeared to be smirking. What does he want? Why is his behavior so inconsistent?

Operator Seven's condition improved and she returned to cutting hair. Nevertheless, discussions about her mental health do go on, especially as she claimed someone has been driving by her house at night and honking the horn. It is difficult for her to sleep and she doesn't like to cut hair when she is tired. She doesn't seem to have enough energy to iron her smock. It looks disgraceful, and she has started smoking.

The dog will not let up and has taken to cutting out articles regarding the anti-haircutting lobby. The edges of the articles are usually ragged as he has a difficult time managing the scissors. He sticks the pieces in Operator Seven's chair or tapes them to her mirror when he can get a boost up. A new development—Operator Seven has some articles of her own. They report that salons all over the country are proudly advertising haircuts.

This news has sent the dog over the edge. He has attached himself to Operator Seven's leg with his teeth. Operator Seven seems unaffected, she is cutting more hair than ever before. To avoid tripping on the dog, she must swing her leg in a wide arc as she walks. The beast slides along on his flank, eyes rolled back in his head like a shark.

We have asked her, "Are you in pain?" "Can you not shake the beast off?" "How can you tolerate this?"

"The teeth," she mutters, "never break the skin."

Carole Maso

Sappho Sings The World Ecstatic

Carole Maso is the author of *AVA, Ghost Dance, The Art Lover,* and *The American Woman in the Chinese Hat.*

Sappho Sings the World Ecstatic

Beached on the hypnotic, lilting lip of a sweet— of a sweet
young nymph's clitoris, Sappho sings the world delirious...
Haloed, rosy—

> May I say
> *I think no girl—*

She sings, on that delicious precipice, longing, hip, the
world—holds in her mouth: word and rosy pearl and world.
Sweet apple. Violet breasted. Aureole...

> May I say
> *I think no girl—*

Between morning and afternoon, sweet apple and rosy
pearl, light and light and hip and cliff and thighs. Dripping,
honey, lilting, sweet, Sappho dreams hypnotic, sea, waves at
her hips, between the lovely legs delirious of a gorgeous
nymph. She sucks the luscious aureole, the world, she sings on
that delicious precipice: *I shall go unleashed, unpegged.* The
beach is wide. The world is round ecstatic.

Dizzied Sappho dreams the key in medium miraculous,
she sees a girl, a gorgeous word, a world, she reaches:

On a deserted seashore a girl is being beached. It takes a
long time, and instead of a back and forth motion, the waves
pull only out and the tide goes visibly out. At the same time, the
girl, without moving, seems higher and higher up on the shore.
She watches the sea desert her with inactive longing, accepting

the sand, as she dries off, which slowly collects around her. Idly she watches a bird fly long across the sky.

Says: Maya. Sappho having fallen into a fever dream and lingering. In a medium unknown at the lip of the hypnotic word and Maya, key, asleep. At the lip of the beach over a perfect woman covered. Ecstatic Sappho moans and reaches in slow motion, her hand, stranded. At the mercy of—
Bird and sea and dream ecstatic. Whispers: Maya. At the mercy of —
Maya Deren. *At Land.*
At the mercy of —
At Land. Close-up. She shudders.
At the mercy of miraculous. She conjures the woman Maya, smiles, and who is this?
On that delicious precipice, all is wonder, pearl within her grasp ecstatic. Where, oh where's my pussycat? she wonders. And watches the blonde and black go at it.
Sappho longing dreams the world. She lifts her lyre and sings a gorgeous song and girl ecstatic. She holds a word, a world, a pearl, delirious. Swallow now, a sweet nymph whispers. She sighs, looks up to see a woman in a cocktail dress: crawling across a dining table on all fours toward her desire.
She smiles, swallows, stutters, mounts her like a luscious horse with bridle, saddle, leather crop and sputters *go!* And sputters *oh!* and *fuck!* She sees before her everything: a lovely curved cuneiform of woman, lilting horse and crown and wondrous girl and gallop. Frenzied, frantic: horse of her desire, live forever, oh and fuck and suck and shudder.
"Trembling was all living, living was all loving, someone was then the other one."
In the city of Paris...
And Sappho now is underneath, delirious. Mound and aureole and bound and ridden, shackled there, and blindfolded and tied reminded there of rosy world and cocktail dress and all the place yet to go. She hones her hope, her longing lust, and sung and bound by garlands, strum, encircled, galloped, sucked, she sputters—
Fuck.

At that sweet and perilous delirious. She whispers Maya Deren open mouthed, sings fuck into the lovely, lilting lyre and nymph. Delirious she holds the rosy pearl now in her mouth between teeth and tongue and lips. Encircling the universe she licks, she laps the world ecstatic. Mouth to golden now, mound to mouth she sings: *May I say—*

But sucking loses her way.

May I—

And hip and Paris.

May I say—
I think no girl
that sees the sun
will ever equal you in skill.

She trembles still. She shudders, sputters *fuck* and *skill.*

Delirious and looking up from lip and clitoris and mound she sees the city of Paris lit up. "Trembling was all living, living was all loving, someone was then the other one." The women walk the street syntactic. Sings Paris Paris Paris Paris. A large white poodle dog and walking down the boulevard. Sappho longing dreams the world ecstatic.

We thought that much of what our Sappho saw was lost to us where the papyrus tore but now we see she sees the women, street, the poodle dog and even Maya crawling on the table toward her desire. Lowering herself slowly onto the woman's luscious mouth, her nymph, she lifts her lilting lyre and sings — She's seeing things: a movie screen—the beach is wide a line of white and pearls, a door. In the place where the papyrus tore. She strums her lyre and rolls her hips and shudders, sings, she's seeing things:

. . . *gentle girl. . . sweet apple. . . lavish on me. . . with all that heaven ever meant. . .*

Sappho sings the world eternal. Each word caressed , a pearl. *Because I could not wait. . . Heaven. . .*

On that open mouth.

. . . passion, yes
. . . utterly, can
. . . shall be to me
. . . a face
. . . shining back at me
. . . beautiful
. . . indelibly

Hallucinating in the luminous afternoon, gorgeous beautiful and skill, indelibly she's seeing things: a mouth, a key — she shifts her hips. What is this?

Med. shot: 1st dream girl looking through window, seen from outside (Botticelli shot).
Road, mirror figure walking up, disappears; then dream girl 2 pursuing, arriving at stairs of house, starting up them.
Dream girl 1 drawing key from her mouth.
Her hand holding out the key.

Sappho lusting arches her back ecstatic.

Close up: Girl 2 trying to continue.
Mirror figure (from below) continuing into room, turning to bed.
Girl 2 trying, being tilted away.
Top of stair, her hand grasps banister, pulls herself up.
Mirror figure deposits flower on the bed.
Close up: Girl straining up.
Mirror figure, standing, then disappears.
Girl, as if released from pull, because back to position on stairs.
Another position back, bounced back and back.
Another position back and back.
Another position back and back (7 shots total)
Position forward
Position forward

Position forward
Position forward
Position forward
Position forward

Close up: Girl's face.

She lingers there on face and lost and sputters, hum and girl and straining up and happiness complete unleashed hypnotic.

Position forward. "She came to be happier than anybody else who was living then." Position forward. Sappho has never seen a place of such—

Girl straining up. Crawling delirious toward her desire. "She came to be happier..." In the gorgeous city of Paris. Poodle dog. Yellow flowered hat. Alice Babette. Sappho does not entirely understand how women appear to her from the strings of her lyre:

Hypnotic Maya D and other she has never seen before while on that gorgeous lilting Grecian lip and hip and nymph ecstatic.

Where is my pussycat? She watches the blonde and black go at it. Closes her eyes. Lilting honey lip explore.

Papyrus tore swallow now. . . and mouth and lip and skill and fuck.

Love.

Where the papyrus tore, dissolved, Sappho sings a line of sweet girls in white and gloves and veils and slippers, lilting rose communion clothes. Sappho lying on a bed of thyme and sighing lifts her lyre. A lovely nymph caressing her from behind. Her fingers in her mouth swallow now and suck. A garland woven around her neck. They watch the long white line of young girls open mouthed. Haloed passion aureole. So very, oh so very lovely—singing, sighing makes them so.

Once I saw a very gentle
very little
girl picking flowers.

Golden genet
grew along the shore.

And the ripe girls wore garlands.

Girls with voices like honey.

And the garlands were wild parsley. . .

Long shot:Road: hand deposits flower, disappears.
        Shadow of girl arrives, her hand picks up flower.
        Flower dangling beside girls legs walking.
        Girl's shadow walking, stops, smells flower. . .

Med. shot: Girl's shadow on door, hand knocks, tries door.
        Hands get key from purse, key slips, falls.
        Feet, key dropping on ground, bouncing away.
        Hand, reaching for key, misses, key bounces away.
        Key bouncing down stairs.
        Key bouncing down stairs, followed by feet pursuing.
Close-up: Hand finally catching key.
        Feet going up stairs again.
        Hand with key unlocks door, pushes it open.

Pushes it open. Sappho's thighs are parted, opened by the
woman 6BC and oh and slow and fuck. A bouquet of visions
and flowers and wild. . . A tender key. An open mouth. And they
called the poodle Basket.

Sappho sings the world ecstatic. What lovely turn of
mind, desire has brought this dreamy procession before her
eyes. She sighs. She smiles. And the little girls in their white
dresses gathering flowers.

The girls for once are not ornamental. The girls for once
are not just decorative. Incidental. The girls and their gorgeous
rituals and tenderness which make Sappho honey song and
hum are not for once relegated to one white wig somewhere.
The girls for Sappho are the whole story. Holding their delirious
bouquets and visions, open mouthed.

Sappho sings and sells sea shells. Sappho sings by the

seashore. She rolls the rosy aureole and pearl the world around and round. Sea pearl to pearl with her and lip she shudders honey gold and conjures—this must be Paradise—or maybe Paris. "She came to be happier than anybody else who was alive then." Gorgeous lilting rosy pearl. She rides the woman world syntactic. Sings Paris Paris Paris Paris. And they walk the poodle Basket.

The blonde and black go at it. Ask Sappho finally, How about it Pussycat? On thar delicious precipice, miraculous, delirious. And dreaming Sappho sings and weeps and shudders, stutters—a great appendage now attached! And strapped—and oh and oh and oh and oh and—

Poodle dog ecstatic!

A rosy line of girls in white communion clothes. She reaches for the key unleashed. A halo. Open door. And hip unhinged. The girls for once are the whole story. The blond and black go at it. Gallop!

Pearl to pearl to pulsing pearl she drags her tongue and teeth a little, throbbing ripe and slower, shudder. She sucks the rosy pearl ecstatic. Girly girl. She sees the sea and shoulder, slower, shells. And yellow flowers grew there gentle. She licks her salty lips and sucks eternal. The little girls all in a row—Sappho's singing makes it so.

She sees a woman now against a door (Papyrus tore). Blue. Blue door. Stutters. Shudders. I adore. She crawls, adores, on all fours toward her desire. Syllable by syllable. Word by word by word.

My beauty love, Sappho dreams, adores, in the place the papyrus tore.

And Sappho sees:

Med. shot: Two girls sitting across from each other with
the sea in the background.

Same shot, very still, without movement.

Face of blond talking animatedly, pan down
along her arm which
moves figures on chess board; hold on chess
board until another hand comes in; pan up to
brunette talking animatedly.

Chess board with alternate pieces being moved

at rapid rhythm. chess moves:
17 WKt-Q5
17 B Q x P
18 W B-Q6
18 B Q x R ch
19 W K-K2
19 B B x R

She marvels at the specificity of her 20 B K-Q3 desire:

Blonde talking animatedly then pan to brunette talking;
then pull back to show both on one side of the board
leaning their heads back and as camera continues to pull
back reveals her caressing hair of girls.
20 W P-K5
20 B Kt-QR3
21 W Kt x P ch
Their faces laughing, leaning back.
Her face laughing.
Over her shoulder everyone laughing, their arms
reaching forward and moving chess pieces without
looking.
21 B K-Q
22 W Q-B6 ch

What lovely world is this that Sappho conjures in desire?
BK-Q and P-K5. Everything within her grasp. The world is vast,
a pearl, hypnotic. She crawls on hands and knees toward word
and world and rosy pearl and sea eternal.

Where oh where's my Pussycat? Where's my Poodle
Dog? And Maya Deren on all fours. [Shot B-7.]

Sappho longs and loves the world.

And Alice Babbette, petite crevette. On the Rue Christine
after the war. Adore. Picking flowers gentle. Rose is a rose is a
rose eternal and I am because my little dog knows me.

She wanders gorgeous key syntactic. Violet-breasted.
Poodle Basket.

The Black and Blonde at Chess

Suddenly, she is no longer holding the stones but is standing there watching two girls sitting over a chess board playing. They seem gay about it, talking to each other as they do so. Then she is standing in back of them, because they are suddenly both on one side of the board and she begins stroking their hair. They love it and lean their heads back like cats and begin to laugh with delight and she, stroking their hair laughs too. The chess game goes on although they do not seem to play very seriously. Nevertheless the white queen is about to be taken and as the black haired one moves a figure to knock off the white queen, the girl suddenly stops stroking their hair, grabs the queen, and begins to run.

She grabs the queen. She pets the cat. She pets the queen. She goes unleashed. She holds the key. A rosy haloed line of girls in white begin to sing. And that of course is everything. She rolls and sucks the rosy pearl. She holds the key, the word, the world, and sings ecstatic.

Shot lists from Maya Deren's "Meshes of the Afternoon," and "At Land." Italicized verse is Sappho. Quotations are from Gertrude Stein.

Kat Meads

In The Guise Of An Explaination Of My Aunt's Life

Kat Meads was born in North Carolina and now lives in California. She has published a poetry collection titled *Filming the Everyday*, and her fiction has appeared in *Short Fiction by Women, Kiosk*, and other magazines. A one-act play she wrote was produced in Kansas in 1995.

In the Guise of an Explanation of My Aunt's Life

#1

For the sake of believability, suppose:
—this is not an imagined life but a lived one
—that all happened exactly as described, no additions or subtractions
—that we deal here with pure plot
—that no family member objected to the exposure of internal secrets or assaulted the author, face to face, with how-dare-you-tell wailings
—that this family assumed all families cheated on taxes, disliked their children, killed squawking chickens bare-handed, ate calf brains with pleasure
—that they accepted with humor and grace the sad but universal banality of all deviance, rendering the concept of secrecy bogus, understanding this page reveals nothing a hundred pages written by a hundred others have not already revealed, reducing the idea of family secret to the level of a bad knock-knock joke, wherein "Who's There?" will be answered in this instance by the personality "Sister."

She has a less generic name, my Aunt Sister. It is Selena, her mother's name, bestowed and avoided by that mother, eight brothers and sisters, a slew of aunts, uncles and cousins and, in time, by a slew of nieces and nephews. Sister of, sister to, identification by kinship: it could work on a mind, nurture a grudge, fashion a tale of childhood grievance stoked by adolescence, marriage and motherhood.

Sixty-two and three-quarters she was when the lid blew

off, more than sixteen thousand days of cooking-cleaning-toenail clipping-monthly bleeding behind her. Like hail stones in summer came those rat-a-tat-tat shrieks. They bounced off the kitchen walls, kitchen floors; they bounced along with pots and pans. Even Uncle Ferris the Self-Absorbed deserted his recliner to stare, slack-jawed with amazement, while his lanky wife, my Aunt Sister, known primarily for her ingratiating giggle, systematically annihilated their habitat.

A Brother's View

"I went because Ferris called. Said Sister was tearing up the kitchen, ripping into curtains, breaking plates. Said 'you gotta come up here and help me, James. Every time I edge past the refrigerator, she raises the frying pan. You gotta come, She'll listen to you.'

"Frankly I tried to get out of it. 'Ferris,' I said, 'I don't want to get in your husband-wife squabbles. She's my sister, but she's your wife.' Then I heard what sounded like a pig's squeal and decided maybe he was right for once. Maybe he did need another set of hands. Sister's awful good with a butcher knife.

"I got there in ten minutes, maybe five, knocked on the door because you don't go barging into anybody's house, not even your sister's, without giving some warning. After a while I just followed the noise. There she was, just like Ferris described her, wild and raving, tearing up what was left of curtains she sewed herself, running out of whole things to break. And there stood Ferris, holding out his hands, pleading: 'Honey, now, honey, you gotta stop this now. You keep this up, somebody's gonna get hurt.'

"'*Do* something,' he says when he sees me, so I walked on into the kitchen, hands in my pockets. You got sense, you don't lunge at a kicking mule. She asked what in the hell I was doing there. First time I remember Sister cursing me or anybody. I pretended I'd stopped by on the way back from Bartock. 'You're a damn liar,' she said, the bow of her apron twisted around front, hair kind of electrified. 'Ferris called you.'

"'No I didn't, I didn't,' Ferris starts to whine, but I said straight out: 'He did. And with good cause, looks to me.' Her hands were still twitching, like the race was over but it had been a long one. I took a chance and told her to look around, see what she'd done. After a while she bent down to pick up a cup handle. 'I'm fine now,' she said, her back to me. 'I appreciate you coming by, but I'm fine now.'"

A Husband's View

"Well she went absolutely crazy, that's all there was to it. She wasn't Sister. She wasn't my wife. I tell you she could have killed me and not even realized what she'd done. I tried everything to calm her. Coaxing, promising I'd drive straight to town and bring home that new sewing machine she wanted. I was a desperate man; desperate men promise desperate things. She was destroying the kitchen, all our dishes. We were going to have to replace every saucer and plate. The whole linoleum floor was covered with glass, and she standing in the middle of it, gashes up and down her arms. James was a fool to walk in there like he did. He can say now it was nothing because nothing happened, but it could have. Just watching almost finished me: my pulse was racing, I was covered with sweat. My heart could have given out at any time. It certainly could have."

The View of God or a Ceiling Fly

The crown of a gray-headed female. One set of unpainted toes thrust forward, peeking from a sandal strap. A twelve-inch circle of boiling water.

In the adjoining room spider-shaped Ferris, stretched on the recliner, stick arms and legs stuck to a belly swell.

Back in the kitchen: minute after minute of nothing more lively than a freckled arm, bent at the wrist, competently stirring the cauldron before it boiled.

But Why Did It Boil?

True or useless historical clues:

As a young child Sister smacked her favorite doll silly, grabbed her own earlobes and spun like a top to make herself "see stars." (Source: family lore.)

She liked to kill snakes, especially vipers, with a butcher knife, eye to lidless eye, none of that sneaking up from behind stuff.

She gave birth to a daughter teachers declared a genius, a passion flower with a twenty-one-inch waist who raced off with the first substantial set of muscles, the first Vitalis-trained spit curl, who offered a ride.

Other Suspicious/Contributing Characteristics

The giggle—low pitched, unconscious, spontaneous, the tic that followed funny remarks, not so funny remarks, silence.

The hair—forty years of the same below the ears, side part, curl-as-it-might style.

The good sport attitude—not a blip of envying wives with other husbands, mothers with other daughters, the richer, the less harassed, the better loved.

The excellent cook reputation—her renowned ability to feed twelve farm hands at twelve noon twenty dishes piping hot: fried ham, fried pork, fried chicken, fried gravy, butter beans, string beans, Navy beans, cabbage, squash, rutabaga, sweet potatoes, stewed corn, corn fritters, corn bread, spoon bread, lemon pie, apple pie, chocolate cake, yellow cake, sugared tea.

...And all this before Uncle Ferris permanently retired to the recliner, counting his heart beats, terrified if Sister stepped marginally from view. All this before their carefree but penniless daughter dropped off her late-in-life love child for Sister to raise.

Tempting to conclude Aunt Sister sniffed all that coming in the steam of boiling corn late July, late morning. Tempting to think she decided right then and there:

"If I'm ever going to cut loose, spin totally out of control, I gotta do it now."

From the Eye of the Storm

"The corn was boiling on the stove. Eight ears, I counted. Have you ever taken a good close look at an ear of corn? All those nubby rows. Not always even, but line after line. Ferris, he likes young, sweet corn, pale white and tiny kernels. I like mine yellow and overgrown. Then your teeth can chomp; they don't have to mince. I had a pork roast in the oven. Just Ferris and me eating that day, the kitchen hot from the stove and me feeling like a fat old copperhead. You know how they look when they're sunning—thick and dreamy, like they don't have the energy to fang a minnow?"

Or:

She gets caught up in the swirl of the corn, in the numbers of corn kernels. She thinks maybe she didn't make enough.

Ferris is always hungry on Fridays, she doesn't know why. He is.

A tiny dot of hot water splatters on her hand. She thinks: that was nothing, not even close to a wasp sting. Then the contradiction: yes, it was something; it sure as hell *was*.

The first glass gets knocked by accident as she reaches for the dish towel; the rest she breaks on purpose, hitting stride midway through the second cabinet, certain that the plates and pans are flying off the shelves to meet her. After a while the sound of that shattering needs a partner—something human but just. She molds that second sound from scratch, digging deep inside her rib cage, pumping those lungs like an accordion. She's screeching, running around in circles. She can do both at once, like the trick of rubbing your head and patting your stomach. She can do it. She can. She is.

A Choice of Morals
—never assume continuity
—a routine life's routineness is defined by its surprises
—all is accident, nothing preordained.

Mea Culpa

Aunt Sister's first-person paragraph is improvised. What choice did I have, stuck with a main character who's not talking, whose muteness has subverted the very theme from *secrets* to *secrecy*?

Come on, Sister. Spill your guts.

What about the first midnight you looked hard, really hard, at the spider sharing your bed?

What about the first hour you noticed that gray-haired, stoop-shouldered stranger giggling back from mirror glass?

What about the spinning moment that spun no stars?

What about the second you slipped through your mama's hole and the bedside crowd exhaled that exasperated, dismissive, familial sigh: "Another girl, another girl"?

Tell us, Sister, do.

The plot is itching to know.

Elisabeth Sheffield

Sugar Smacks

Elisabeth Sheffield's stories have appeared in *Asylum Arts Annual, The Ledge, Gulf Coast,* and *Southern Plains Review.* Currently she's working on a novel and teaching at the University of Illinois at Chicago.

Sugar Smacks

She left this morning, letting the door slam behind her. She did not say when she would be back. The decision to withhold this information was most likely a punishment for nocturnal failures. To be somewhat more explicit—she has high standards for performance in the bedroom which last night were not met. The inability to rise to these standards was probably the result of excessive alcohol consumption before retirement—specifically two bottles of Wild Irish Rose. The wine was consumed in secret because this particular vintage is only fit for derelicts and persons of low social standing. It would of course be impossible to inform her that this is precisely why this wine and not a more refined one was consumed—for the purpose of self abasement. The idea was that through the imbibition of this plebeian beverage, the self would come to feel as low as it actually is in her presence. In other words, it was hoped that a concordance, via the concord grape, would be created between mind and body. Unfortunately the attempt to humble the self in her honor was overdone—one glass of wine led to another and another so that by bedtime, two one liter bottles of Wild Irish Rose had been emptied and the libido was as limp as a dead flower.

Perhaps she will not return for many hours; in fact it would not be surprising if she does not return until tomorrow. It has long been suspected that she has a lover—perhaps more than one. There is evidence... First of all, the pictures of strange men in her wallet. If questioned, she would probably say that they are her brothers but the startling degree of genetic variation, from round blue Caucasian eyes to narrow dark Oriental ones for instance, would invalidate this claim. But then perhaps her mother had a number of lovers. However, if this was the case then it only provides more support for the theory of infidelity since it is more than likely that the maternal predilection for seminal variety has been inherited by the daughter. And then there are the phone calls. Sometimes the voices ask for her by name; at other times they claim to have reached the wrong number. The ruse is of course obvious.

However, but for such occasional flashes of resentment, her infidelities are borne patiently. There is no reason after all why better treatment should be expected. The services rendered are for the most part unsatisfactory—not only in the sexual category, but other areas as well. The other day, for example, an attempt was made to carry the groceries to the car. A grocery cart was discarded in favor of the arms in order to demonstrate their muscular strength. Unfortunately milk from a leaking carton had begun to seep through the bottom of one of the bags. The hands tried desperately to cover the disintegrating paper as a child clutches at its crotch to keep from urinating but in the end nothing could prevent the cascade of groceries to the ground. Bright red strawberries tumbled out of a green cardboard carton, disappeared under the wheels of a passing car and then reappeared, wet as wounds or stigmata on the black asphalt; cans of albacore and tins of smoked oysters rolled across the parking lot, bouncing off the wheels of shopping carts, throwing themselves in front of the feet of passers by as if asking to be kicked; as the quivering contents of a broken jar of plum preserves dissolved with shame in a puddle of milk. Imagine the mortification, mirrored twice in the round lenses of her sunglasses—a man stooping over a pool of jam laced milk, like a dog cowering in its own urine.

No, given such a record, resentment of her is untenable and so a vent for hostility must be found. And in fact an excellent source of relief has been discovered in aerobic activity. Exercise exorcises the body of the toxic byproducts of resentment, dissolves the corrosive chemical waste of even the most rancorous heart. Which this one to be sure is not—the most rancorous of hearts, that is. For while it is often thought that she fails to temper justice with mercy, it is understood that her cruelty has the same effect as a run in oxygen deficient air: it helps to build the strength of cardiac tissue.

Unfortunately oxygen deficient air is hard to come by at sea level, where residence has been established. A facsimile of such conditions can be achieved, however, by placing cotton balls in the nostrils. Partial blockage of the nasal passages helps to place a strain on the circulatory system such that the heart tightens in the chest, sometimes even constricting the flow of blood to the brain so that leopard spots of darkness dapple the field of vision. Usually the cotton is inserted in front of the bathroom mirror, in order to admire the sensual effect of distension on the thin, beakish nose that along with a chain of department stores comprises the paternal inheritance.

After cotton has been inserted in the nasal apertures, the bedroom is retired to in order to put on the rest of the aerobic accessories. These include a Pendleton buttondown, slightly tight in the shoulders (the irritating effect of the wool fibers on the skin promotes a virtuous glow), snug fitting Levis firmly secured at the waist with a thick leather belt (spandex does not sufficiently mortify the few pounds of excess lipotissue in the abdomen), and an ancient pair of tennis shoes with soles hardly thicker than paper (to better understand the path that is traveled).

Outside, the sun scourges the balding pate, lashes the back and shoulders with its sizzling rays, mercilessly driving forward the legs that are already leaden even though only seven miles of the usual route have been covered. And as the sun urges the body on to the end of its route, to shade and rest, the fingertips throb and the hard rubber tips of the tennis shoes abrade the swollen toes. The outside world seems flimsy, unreal as coils of heat distorted-air rise up from the asphalt and wring the flesh, soaking the clothes with perspiration, blurring the vision with salty tears that make the shapes of houses, trees, automobiles and people as soft as pieces of tissue. For this reason, it is perhaps quite some time before the presence of the other, running alongside the self, is felt.

The first thing to penetrate consciousness is the sound of

his breath, an irregular rasping like the sound of a file shaping a long, pointed fingernail. But when the head at last turns to look at him, it is seen that the nails of the hand he raises in greeting are bitten to the pinkish quick. The second thing that catches the attention, though half obscured by a flop of curly blond hair, are his eyes—blue and round and wet as something that is still very young. Yes his eyes are round and wet like the eyes of something that still glistens with uterine fluids but his face is another story altogether: his pale, yellowish complexion is fissured with wrinkles, rough and weathered as the hull of some old boat. He pushes the flop of hair back from his forehead and grins, displaying a set of gleaming white teeth as the skin at the corners of his eyes crinkles and reveals the fossil record of too many days spent at the beach during youth.

And as he smiles his breath becomes harsher, more labored, so that the sound of the air dragging over the parched membranes of his throat is truly painful to hear. The eyes turn back to the path before them, refusing to look anymore at this ghastly white smile bobbing along over the sidewalk, but his breath continues to saw away at the ears and his presence must at last be acknowledged.

Reluctantly, the head is once again turned in his direction. Go away, he is told.

Can't, he wheezes. This is... like... my route.

Then pull ahead.

Would if I... could... man, he replies. Then he points at the front of his sweat-soaked t-shirt, to the center of his bony breast and nods.

His gesture is met with a stare.

It's like a... congestion of... butter, he explains. The freeway...rush hour...in my arteries... heart attack city.

The only choice is to run faster. The legs, heavy with fatigue, are forced to lengthen their stride, while the arms, chafed raw at the pits by the Pendleton buttondown, are pumped harder to increase forward momentum. His heaving breaths grows fainter and fainter, like the sound of a tug-boat disappearing in the night.

Each step now sends a lance of pain from the big right toe through the foot and up the leg. Undoubtedly this is due to the formation of a blood blister on the pad of the toe and so there is no need to stop and inspect the foot. Further, proof of the existence of the blood blister will be received when the skin breaks, which it invariably does, without removing the tennis shoe. First, there will be a sudden sensation of wetness and then the canvas toe, rusty with old dried blood, will be revivified with red.

In the meantime, the pain recalls a childhood favorite— the story of the Little Mermaid who felt as if "a thousand knives" were cutting into her legs at every step. Paternal authority forbid the fairy tale— on the grounds that it was for girls—and so it was perused with the door locked while wobbling back and forth across the room in a pair of very small and pointed high heels pilfered from the shoe department of one of the familial emporiums. Back and forth, back and forth until daggers of pain stabbed the toes and raked the calves and a kind of kinship with the Little Mermaid had been achieved through physical anguish.

And then suddenly the mind is summoned out of its reverie by an all too familiar sound, that painful chug like an engine about to die. The head turns in spite of itself to confirm what it already knows—that he is back. He stares straight ahead with flat, round eyes, his yellow face gleaming with the brine of his own perspiration, his mouth open, making convulsive circles for air. It is brought to his attention that he has a bad heart, or so he has claimed.

True, he wheezes. Very true. It's like so... genuine... of you... to take an interest, he adds, but he doesn't stop. Rather, he pushes on, his bony chest thrust forward, cutting through his own pain—for he must be experiencing severe physical discomfort at this point—like the prow of a ship slicing through the water. It is really quite impressive, the way he asserts mind over body and sails his feeble vessel through the waves of anguish. At this point it must be admitted that something like admiration is felt. And so, perhaps against the better judgement, an invitation is issued—to come over, at the end of his run, for a glass of beer.

His lips seem to attempt to form a reply—drawing together, parting, then closing and opening again—but nothing resembling speech sounds issues forth. Finally he raises his right hand, making a circle with his forefinger and thumb, while at the same time vigorously nodding his head.

Matt (this is the name that has been disclosed) has demonstrated his superiority as a runner beyond a doubt—exhibited a degree of stamina and self-abnegation that has perhaps raised him to the level of the aerobic aristocracy—and so a noble repast is prepared for him as he waits in the garden, drinking a beer. Foie gras on a bed of butter lettuce, circled by a line of deviled eggs, rich yellow centers spilling over the firm whites like a cascade of gold coins; a treasury of assorted pastries, flaky with fat; a glass plate of tender pink shrimp accompanied by a bowl of freshly made mayonnaise sauce; and another bottle of imported beer. Before this feast is carried out to the garden, the toilet is carefully prepared in the bathroom: a hot shower so as not to offend his nostrils with the byproducts of the bacteria that have fed on the body's secretions; styling product in the hair to achieve an appearance of sleek docility; a trimming of offensive nostril hairs. In the bedroom, black pants are donned along with a crisp white shirt. This outfit is completed in the kitchen by the draping of a clean white towel over the arm. At last there is nothing to do but pick up the silver tray of food and step out onto the patio.

But as the tray is carried outside it is seen that the chaise lounge next to the potted jade tree is empty, the bottle of beer resting on the cement beside it, untouched. A big black fly lands on a deviled egg as the tray is set down beside the beer. It is brushed away and the white towel is drawn over the refreshments to prevent further contamination when a small popping noise is heard in the far corner of the grounds. The gaze shifts to the direction of the sound, the back left corner of the garden and lands on the bright yellow spot of his nylon running shorts: he is on his knees in the dirt, crouched amongst the rose bushes. Slowly the way is made across the lawn, the footfalls sinking into the thick close grass. As the garden is neared, an inquiry is made concerning the nature of his activity.

Evidently this question startles him—he totters and falls forward, arms open, into the roses. He rests there for a moment, his chest pressed against the straining bush, and then he slowly rocks back on the balls of his feet in an attempt to release himself from this uncomfortable embrace. There is nothing to do but assist him, to help him disengage the thorns from his yellowish flesh. And as each thorn is forced to relinquish its small sharp grip, a bright bead of blood adorns his skin, as imperiously red as her thick-painted lips. Thus it is not surprising when he issues his command:

Don't worry, man. It's like totally... superficial. Nothing a little isopropyl alcohol won't take care of.

The rubbing alcohol is located with some difficulty. It is finally discovered lying on its side in the dust at the back of the cabinet beneath the bathroom sink. To further complicate matters, the head is smashed on the top of the door frame as it is withdrawn, summoning up a bump as pink, as prominent as buttocks poised for punishment. There is no time, however, to further examine this injury for his needs must be attended to.

Matt is still in the far corner of the garden. As he is approached for the second time, the source of the popping noise heard earlier is discovered: he is exterminating snails. He plucks one from the roots of a rose bush and its glistening foot retracts into its mottled brown shell as it feels itself become airborne.

They're like... ravishing your roses, he says as he draws his arm back and hurls the snail against the fence. The shell cracks on impact and the exposed body, splayed against the wood, shimmers pearly gray in the afternoon sun. It is an iridescent wetness, oozing like a tear from the seam of a tightly closed lid, like a dribble of saliva from the corner of a mouth agape with lust or pain, seeping into the wood like perspiration stains, the damp infiltration of anxiety and anticipation...

Listen it's mass murder, it's like genocide in the garden, what these guys do to plants man. I mean I'm... prostrated if they're like your pets but I was only trying to help, to express appreciation for your fine hospitality.

His words are muffled by revery as a mother's voice is diminished by the closed door of her adolescent son's bedroom but finally they penetrate consciousness. Oh no, he is told, his assistance is gratefully accepted; in fact it is an honor to entertain a guest with such an extensive knowledge of horticulture. Later, it is suggested, after his wounds have been attended to and refreshment has been taken, he can provide further instruction.

Unfortunately, the repast that was prepared with such care and attention does not meet his approval. As it is set down before him on the glass top of the patio table, he pulls back in his chair. Please, that's like too... sublime..., he says, waving the food away with a yellow hand. A glass of tap water—maybe a few potato chips. Stale is fine.

This request for stale potato chips will first necessitate a shopping trip (the problem of how to achieve the requisite staleness will have to be dealt with later). Such a trip will involve a walk on pain swollen feet across the parking lot (site of the recent shopping bag humiliation), down the over-stocked aisles where products packaged in savage greens, glaring reds, and vicious yellows assail the senses and brand names like BOLD, SHOUT, and SUGAR SMACKS besiege the sensibility, where bright white lights interrogate the flesh, mercilessly exposing every follicle, every pore, up to the cashiers and their relentless conveyor belts. A trickle of perspiration is oozing down the neck, slowly slithering over the skin like the foot of a snail as this ordeal is contemplated, when suddenly a thought comes hurtling out of nowhere and splatters into revelation: perhaps it does not matter if she does not return.

More and more it is no longer a concern if she does not come back. And if she does her things may very well be waiting in the foyer, packed in the leopard print luggage that was given to her for her birthday. Increasingly it is recognized that life with her was probably a tedious affair, more predictable than the most menial job. Her desires were most likely as banal, as common as a garden variety daisy, her needs scarcely more than elemental. Satisfying Matt, on the other hand, in such a way as to ensure his happiness would undoubtedly be a challenging task, requiring, like the cultivation of exotic species of flora and fauna, painstaking research and scrupulous attention.

The other day, for instance, five bags of potato chips were wasted in the attempt to achieve a facsimile of staleness. The first two attempts, which involved holding the chips in a colander over a pot of boiling water, produced a briny mash. Finally, inspiration struck and it was thought to put the chips in the bathroom while the shower was running. The first trial was a failure although the results were an improvement over the boiling water method. The second trial, however, was a complete success, producing chips with both integrity and the required softness.

At this point, in fact, the technique has been perfected and it is now possible to produce stale potato chips within a matter of minutes. These are placed in a bowl on the silver tray, along with a wine glass and a bottle of Evian and carried out to the patio, where it has become customary to retire after the daily run together. Today, however, like that first day, he has disappeared—the patio is once again tantalizingly deserted. From the far right corner, just past the chaise lounge where his damp black t-shirt lies crumpled in a ball, the lawn is surveyed. The gaze sweeps over the rose bushes along the fence, hangs for a minute in the back right corner of the lawn until it is ascertained that there is no movement in the trembling shade of the jacaranda tree, picks up again and carefully scans the other side of the patio along the left wing of the house, probing between the clay pots of yellow Hawaiian hibiscus, penetrating the green tendrils of the hanging plants to investigate the shadows along the white stucco wall. Nothing stirs except for twigs and leaves—rifled by the light wind that is blowing in from the ocean—and after a moment more of searching it must be acknowledged that he is gone.

And then a sound is heard, coming from the other side of the wood fence behind the point of observation—a whirring noise, followed after a moment or two by light girlish laughter. The salver is placed on the cement so that the hands can unlatch the gate in the fence that opens to a path between the high green hedge and the garage. Stepping past the tiger lilies alongside the garage, the body turns the corner into the driveway just as the laughter ascends into a shriek of surprising strength considering its source—a small girl in a lime green dress astride what appears to be the old exercise bicycle that had been stored in the garage. She screams an aria of childish delight, the sunlight cavorting on her bobbing red curls, the breeze flirting with her flared skirt to reveal black spandex biking shorts as her feet, though they barely reach the pedals, pump energetically. And beneath her bare white legs, his palms pressed against her calves, the whining pedals almost brushing against him, lies Matt.

As the bicycle is approached from the shadows alongside the garage, the little girl's laughter fades like the singing of birds before a storm, and her legs cease their pumping. The empty pedals spin beneath her black sandal clad feet as the lime dress flutters limply over her dangling thighs. It takes a moment or two for him to realize that her calves have gone slack in his hands, that the pedals are spinning of their own accord, that his pleasure has more or less been terminated. Finally, as the shadows of the footrests come to a stop over the upper portion of his face, his eyes open. They blink, as blankly blue as a swimming pool in the mask of shadow and then he slowly slides from under the bicycle and stands up, brushing the dirt off his yellow shorts.

Could I like borrow five bucks? I never carry cash over the pain barrier. It's a whole other... realm.

His request is met with some incredulity but the wallet, still damp with perspiration, is withdrawn from the Levis and the amount solicited subtracted and handed over. He turns around and gives it to the girl who has in the meantime slid off the bicycle. She rolls the bill, bends down to stick it in her black anklet and then leaps up and runs down the driveway, her little shoes snapping at the asphalt .

He watches her disappear down the shady street, pushing his flop back off his forehead, letting his hand rest for a moment on the top of his head. At last he turns around. His expression is without doubt one of profound satisfaction and yet it is difficult to find empirical evidence for this content-ment. Aside from the gleaming white grin he seems to possess no emotional signifiers and thus when he is not smiling his yellow face appears inscrutable. And yet it is beyond doubt that he is delighted, beyond doubt that he has exploited another to purchase his pleasure. This however is to be expected, and has in fact been the order of things for a very long time. The role throughout life has been to provide others with the resources for gratification—this has been the situation from earliest childhood. One of the first memories, for instance, is of using the weekly allowance to buy a can of orange pop for the little boy next door. The day was very hot and dry, the sort of day where it almost hurts to breath and he drank the whole thing down, his plump hands tight around the moisture-beaded cylinder, never offering a sip of the sweet, tangy liquid. Nor was one requested even though the purchase of the soda drained the financial resources for the remainder of the week. But how could he know this—that now the the pockets were as empty, as spent, as the soda can his small lips had so eagerly sucked dry?

The boyhood companion could not have known this anymore than she could have known that her infidelities (for surely those men in her wallet were her lovers) and other cruelties had nearly drained away the capacity to feel. Yes at that point, the day of her departure, something like a condition of emotional penury had been reached. Thus her announce-ment that morning that she could no longer bear the role she had been forced to play did not elicit the response she was surely looking for: the quick, concerned inquiry, the indefati-gable search to sniff out the trouble. "The role she had been forced into...": there was no energy to pursue the meaning of this puzzling statement or even to follow the clicking of her stiletto heels down the driveway. The reaction was as feeble as an exhausted bloodhound, as limp as a tail too spent to wag.

But it is not the lackey's place to indulge in lachrymose tales of abuse. Doubtless the treatment received was thor-oughly justified by the baseness of the recipient... And doubt-less Matt too will leave unless better service is provided. His needs, however degrading to the self, must be attended to.

With these thoughts in mind, he is invited, humbly, even meekly, back into the garden. And as he is followed over the path alongside the garage, past the tigerlilies and through the gate, sunlight spills over the high green hedge and irradiates his blond pompadour, turning it into a crown of gold.

The silhouettes of the palms stand attentively against the orange black night sky, like soldiers awaiting orders. From a chair drawn before the window, the gaze is directed out over the lawn, but the ears are pricked to receive sound vibrations from within the house. Earlier, as Matt was served his post-aerobic chips and water, it was discovered that he is about to be evicted from his apartment, having failed to provide sufficient funds to cover the monthly rental fee. It was suggested that he relocate to this abode. He was amenable although he was initially under the impression that his residence would be conditional upon the performance of housework and other menial tasks. A strange misconception... He did not seem to understand that his presence in itself would be payment enough.

A noise is heard, as stealthy as a pen dragging over a page—the sound of the sliding doors to the patio. A large pale shape emerges from beneath the awning, moves towards the center of the lawn, gradually becomes defined as Matt who, it appears, has pulled the bed sheet around his shoulders. He stops, and gripping the sheet with his hands, spreads his arms so that only the back of his head can be seen above the blank square of cotton. A breeze stirs the sheet and it ripples theatrically. Watching him, a shiver of anticipation runs down the spine: perhaps this is the beginning of a much richer and more original drama, with more subtly defined characterization and a greater variety of scenes than the one participated in until recently. For this new theater of cruelty, such tired props as blood-red lipstick and spike heeled shoes will prove inadequate: the furrows of pain will turn out to be as simple, as inexplicable, as the ridges of a potato chip.

Suddenly the stillness is broken, the blank silence of the lawn splattered by a familiar girlish giggle as the little cyclist bursts through the gate and dances out onto the moonlit lawn.

The guest sinks to his knees, draws the sheet over his head as she begins to kick him, punch him and nip him, with a laugh as merry as the sound of a can of albacore bouncing across a parking lot, as delightful as degradation. And he lets her, accepts her calculated kicks, her flirtatious punches and pretty pinches, as his body begins to convulse and his moans rise up from under the sheet swelling like sails in the balmy night air. Yes his moans swell like sails in the night air as he navigates his pleasure to its final destination beneath the storm of her childish blows and it is simply unbelievable that he would do this, strains credulity that he would abuse my hospitality in this way, that he would use my lawn as the stage for his hackneyed production of pedophilia.

I push back my chair and run down the stairs and as I burst out onto the lawn the girl leaps up and dashes away. He continues to groan beneath the sheet, once again so caught up in his voyage that he fails to notice that the little rat has jumped ship and he's sailing completely alone and so I pick up the hose that the gardener has left in careless coils on the patio, turn the spigot, and direct the cold hard spray at his writhing body. But it is only when the sheet is plastered to his skin, when his arms have come to rest at right angles to his sides and his legs are stretched out before him, perfectly still, that it becomes clear that he will never make me happy.

Diane Goodman

Crimes

Diane Goodman's chapbook of poems, *Constellations*, was published by Heatherstone Press. She has a Ph.D. from Case Western Reserve University, and has work published in an anthology titled *Long Baptism*, as well as in many magazines, including *African American Review*, *Manhattan Poetry Review*, *The Atlantic Review*, and *Indiana Review*. She teaches at Allegheny College.

Crimes

I.
Where you live half a plaster wall, blown out, leaves a space
from where my shoulder would be to my feet, were I standing
there. It looks like a prop for a game, some place to hide your
head behind something under which you'd practice a dangerous limbo, very careful not to scratch your face on the crumbling jagged edge. And there are children crouching at your
feet, smiling into the camera I've sent, thrilled to travel this way
to me.

Over my shoulder my own mother wonders what magazines will pay for a real life photograph like this, where the
stubborn wind had blown fine sand into the new avenues of
your face, where your children's knees are thin and bent as
wishbones.

My mother neglects to notice the ragged children are
wearing t-shirts cut from old nightgowns I wore to death in
college, although my finger traces them all while she talks. And
she does not seem to notice how the light streams in from a
blind wall you wrote has squares cut out of it for air. I think of
rain, wind, the impossibility of protecting yourself from thieves
with guns or knives. I worry for your safety.

II.
One of your children has cut something out of newspaper to
thank me for the small plastic-handled scissors I sent. I think it
is a sun, this flimsy sign that I unfold into its shape, nearly
round with uneven prongs meant to finish in sharp points.

The scissors were an afterthought, set on top of the neatly
folded clothes I found to send you, then safe beneath an Irish

fisherman's sweater that had yellowed evenly to the color of dried corn. In this letter you thanked me, mind-walked me in bad English through your day describing the smell of an open market in the enduring heat that burns and turns you inside out, a heat that taught you to teach your children how to imagine chocolate, to make saliva so they could swallow.

III.

What I hear is your voice calling to children in these photos wearing my old clothes, their strong skin against my once rough and sturdy playthings long gone soft with wear. I imagine you in the Spanish I pay to learn, coaxing them to supper in an easy tongue.

I smell the dinner smells escaping the pot through awkward squares cut in your walls for breeze. It's soup — thin, with clumps of rice and parts of local fish: bones, slippery skin, a stray cloudy eye. You write that when I visit you will serve me this very soup, a staple my people call a delicate.

Delicacy. I dream about that soup, about spoonfuls of it I lift to my mouth without looking. In my dream your smile is a trick designed to make me eat what in my own home would make me sick. Here you are more clever than I know how to give you credit for, having prepared such a delicate soup for me, in thanks for all I've given you.

IV.

What will have happened by the time we finally hold up our hands to wave goodbye?

You will have de-feathered your fattest bird, roasted it with strings of homegrown herbs wound round its headless neck, corn and sturdy peppered bread stuffed up its hollow rump. Together, with your daughters, friends, and strangers, we will have eaten at your table.

Spread across my table now what things I think I'll take. There are hard chocolates I know you will not trust because they're cut and carved like precious stones; their foil wrappers will open for your children like perfect silver stars. And I've bought strong manila paper, new crayons that will not melt, and paper dolls with fold-on summer and winter clothes. But for you, whose endangered smile took me when I found you in a magazine, what can I have? I remember your three tiny girls buckled over like phantoms at your feet, their bare toes crushing the white sand to raise their heels from the steaming ground and I wanted to send you trees, old trees for color and comfort, for shade and the soft sound of blowing wind through so many leaves.

I am preparing to be your guest. This time, I will bring things to take things, the purpose of my visit, finally, to make each other better.

V.

Never have we had glass for these holes cut in our walls for air, so every day brings in our old smell. Except for constant dust and sand, my home is clean. I am used to being able to do nothing.

Why do you come here, though we want you.

My children laugh that you are smaller than they are, that your hair, red snakes in the pictures, is not real. Still, they believe you.

While my sister lived she wrote poems on the cards out mother made from old straw hats too thin to sell, cut squares pressed and flattened without design. Because the student who helps me read your letters will not tell, I will show these cards to you — he says the words are too old.

The wind blows you here today. There is corn cake soaking in honey and I hope I have enough water, that birds won't fly in through the windows at night. My daughters have made you hair combs from wood they found and polished fine, they wait in the road with their gifts and are not afraid.

Laurie Foos

Rescue Fantasies

Laurie Foos received her MFA from Brooklyn College. Her first novel, *Ex Utero*, was published in 1995 by Coffee House Press. Her short stories have appeared in *The Greensboro Review*, *Gulf Coast*, *Beloit Fiction Journal*, and other magazines.

Rescue Fantasies

I am standing naked in the Dead Sea wearing only my watch. It is a Timex with a silver band that has left green rings over my wrist. The horrors of bad metal. I can't be sure if it's the Dead Sea or not—it may very well be the Atlantic —but it feels dead to me so that is what I call it. There is deadness all around in the slosh of the water and the caking mud around my ankles. Even my nipples are puckered and dry.

In the distance I hear my mother crying. She wails, high and sharp, her voice ringing in my ears. I trudge my way up to shore, dragging shells and dead fish under my feet. The fish flake apart as I move them, the skins splitting to expose the whiteness of their guts.

My mother is hungry. The crying doesn't stop.

When I find her she's covered in sand. Her infant body turns blue with wanting. Veins shine through her scalp. I want to ask her what's happened to her body, to her stretch marks, to her station wagon with the rust on the sides. What has happened to her life? But there's no time for that; her hunger is overwhelming. I scrape the seaweed from my breasts and she clamps her mouth on, her eyes closing as I rock her there in the sand.

A dead fish moves between my legs. When I raise my wrist to look at my Timex, I realize it has stopped ticking. There's no telling when she'll be satisfied.

My mother has drowned herself again. A man in a white suit calls to me from the beach to tell me my mother's body has washed ashore. How can he know it's my mother? I wonder, since he'd never seen her before. It is difficult to tell how long we have been on this island. I have lost my Timex and the days pass so slowly.

"It's her, all right," the man says. His face is thick with grief. He removes a dead fish from his lapel and throws it at my feet.

Why must she do this now? I ask the man. I'm having a cocktail party and my mother is the guest of honor. I invite the man to join us if I can fish Mother out and be back for the first round of hors d'oeuvres. The man turns his wrist over as if to look at a watch that is no longer there. He leans close and breathes in my face. His breath smells of dead fish. "I'd do anything for your mother," the man says.

He plants a wet kiss on my cheek and takes my hand. Together we run into the sea where we find Mother face down in the water, her arms spread wide in a dead man's float. I dive down into the water and wrap my arms around Mother's waist. The man lifts her feet and we hoist her out on to the sand. She is naked, her blond hair coiled, her breasts falling to either side of her body.

The man and I kneel down beside her. He pushes down on her stomach; water sprays out her mouth. All the time he keeps looking at his wrist as if he's forgotten he no longer has a watch. I press my mouth to Mother's and blow.

"If she can't be revived, will the party go on?" he asks.

I pinch Mother's nose and stare at him. For a minute I wonder if he is my father, the way he looks at me in his secret way. But then I remember that my father is gone. Besides, I think, my father wouldn't have been caught dead in a white suit.

Just then Mother sits up and clasps her hands over her naked breasts. She shakes her head violently and picks fish scales from her teeth.

"Rebecca," she says, "the party can't go on without me."

She laughs and runs ahead of us, sand flying at her heels. Even though she doesn't thank me for saving her, I can feel her gratitude.

My name is not Rebecca, but I don't have the heart to tell her this. It isn't often that I have the chance to see Mother so spirited.

I'm driving through the South of France in a convertible with the top down. Mother has bought me a shiny new Timex and it glints in the sunlight, throwing light over my face. The highway is open, stretching out before me. I keep driving, though it occurs to me that I have nowhere to go.

The man in the white suit is standing in the middle of the highway waving his arms at me. I slam the brakes, but I'm going so fast there's no telling if I'll stop in time. I push both feet on the brake and close my eyes. The car stops within an inch of the man.

"Madame," he says, as if he's been expecting me, "your mother has run away."

He has a long curling mustache and speaks with a bad French accent. When I ask him how he can be sure of this, he tells me the French police are out looking for her.

"They've issued an APB," he says, "but you're the only one who can find her."

He gets in the car and together we drive down the highway. Everywhere there is green grass and white sand, but Mother is nowhere to be found. She's run away before, I tell him, but has never gotten this far.

"She's always wanted to run away to the South of France," I say. I don't know why I say this. It comes to me as if in a dream.

We reach a coastal town where a festival is being held. There are hundreds of women with babies at their breasts. Their hair is long and they wear no shoes on the hot asphalt. The sight of babies has always lured Mother, I tell the man, parking the car near a sand dune. She can't be very far.

We get out of the car and move into the crowd. I can see his curling mustache through the throngs of women and their screaming babies. I walk past him and glance down at my watch to see how long it's been since I've last seen Mother. It has stopped at twelve o'clock.

A young woman in braids is breastfeeding her infant while sitting on a rock. My heart clenches when I see this. I think of how ravenous Mother must be. The baby sucks and sucks, the mother's eyes closed against the sun.

"Have you seen my mother?" I ask the woman.

The baby opens its mouth and stares at me. The breast

pops free, though the baby continues to suck at the air.

"Oui," the woman says. "She is hiding under this rock."

I brush the woman's skirt aside and climb under the rock. Mother is hunched in a corner with her knees up, sucking her thumb. Her face is streaked with tears.

She wraps her arms around my neck and I lift her up from beneath the rock. With her arms around me, her thumb still stuck in her mouth, I carry her back to the convertible. She settles in the back seat and smiles.

"I was so lost," she says in a mournful voice. "I thought you'd never come for me."

I smooth her hair away from her face and offer her a bottle of milk. She takes it in both hands and drinks from it hungrily, the milk dripping down the front of her blouse.

As I put the car in reverse and start to back away, I look for the man in the white suit. Only after I pull away do I realize he's stolen my watch.

Mother and the man I take to be my father are fighting in the sandbox. They hurl sand in each other's eyes and scream.

"I was here first," Mother whines. "You don't belong."

The man in the white suit and I are trying to make love upstairs in my bedroom. He lies on top of me, thrusting, and I claw at his back. The sounds of Mother's screams fill the air. He nibbles at my ear, but I feel nothing. My watch catches in his hair, pulling at it with silver teeth.

"I've got to see about Mother," I say, pulling away from him.

He lies there on the bed with his erection in the air. He plays with it like a schoolboy, flicking it with his thumbs.

"You don't know what it's like to have a mother," I tell him as I run from the room.

Mother is crying in the sandbox, her hands over her face. Father is sitting with his face averted, his arms folded over his chest. It's been so long since I've seen him that I can't be sure if it's him. Mother turns to me, pointing her long finger in Father's direction. There is sand all over her face.

"Rebecca," she says, "make Daddy say he's sorry."

It seems I've lived this moment a thousand times before.

I step into the sandbox and stand in front of Father with my hands on my hips.

"You mustn't make Mother cry," I say. I can feel my own tears sliding down my face. Hurt Mother, hurt me, I want to say, but I leave it at that.

Father turns to me and gives me a sly wink, as if we're in on some secret. I have no idea what the secret is.

"Ha," he says.

He throws handfuls of sand at us and runs away. I take Mother in my arms and rock her, smoothing her hair with my fingers. The salt of her tears stains the front of my blouse.

"I hate Daddy," she says, and then laughs wildly.

I think of the man upstairs with his erection on the bed. Before I go to him I turn to Mother and whisper in her ear.

"My name is not Rebecca," I tell her.

She claps a hand over her mouth, her eyes wide. She sits cross-legged with her feet buried in the sand.

"Okay," she says with a shrug.

As I walk away I hear it, the faint whispering of a name.

"Mommy," she says, like a taunt.

The doctor tells me I'm pregnant with the child of the man in the white suit. How can he be sure who the father is, I ask him, when he's never even met me?

The doctor lowers his glasses and stares at me.

"It shows," he says. "The smell of dead fish is every-where."

I walk home along the beach, the foam sifting over my feet. A dead fish lands with a splat at the shore line. I think of the first day I saw the man in the white suit, how he seems to have been there every day of my life.

I'll name the baby after him, I think, though his name escapes me.

On the way home I rehearse ways of breaking the news to Mother. I'll tell her I'll call the baby Rebecca, since she seems to like that name. Mother loves babies. Don't you remember the sound of suckling when you ran away to the South of France? I'll say. But I find myself tripping over the words even in rehearsal.

At home I find the man waiting for me in the bedroom

wearing a pair of white boxer shorts. He looks different without the suit, so different I have to look closely to be sure it's really him. I reach my hand inside the shorts and squeeze his erection.

"Sir," I say, because I know of no other name to call him, "we are going to have a child."

His erection falls limp beneath my fingers. He wraps his arms around me and kisses me on the mouth. His breath smells of dead fish.

"Darling," he says, "your mother is hiding under the bed."

He presses a finger to my lips as if to silence me and gives me a worried look. It is the same look he's given me time and time again, even during lovemaking.

I get down on my knees and lift the bedspread. Mother is hanging from the springs, her fingers and toes curved around the metal. Her shoulders heave with her crying; the whole bed shakes. I reach under and grab her by the arm.

"Mother," I say as calmly as I can manage, "the man and I have something to tell you."

She shakes her head violently, her blond hair tangling in the springs. There are seashells stuck in her hair.

"I'll drown myself," she says, and rattles the springs.

I sit cross-legged on the floor for a long time. Is there no pleasing her? I wonder, feeling the flatness of my belly where the baby will be. I have yet to feel like a mother.

I draw in a deep breath and peek at her from under the bedspread.

"But I thought you loved babies," I whisper. My voice echoes through the springs.

Mother crawls out from under the bedspread and buries her head in my chest. Her hair smells like the sea.

"I knew you'd save me," she says.

We sit there for a long time without speaking. The man puts on his white suit and looks down at us. I have doubts about whether or not he'll be a good father.

Mother is threatening to jump off the roof. I hear her screaming as I wash the baby clothes I've bought in preparation for the new arrival. The tiny white baby tee-shirts and diapers glow in the water as if they have a life of their own.

"Rebecca," she screams, "you'd better catch me when I fall."

I drop the baby clothes in the soapy water and run outside. The man in the white suit is making mud pies on the lawn. He motions for me to come forward and hands me the Timex he stole from me in the South of France.

"Your mother needs you," he says. "She'll jump if you're not careful."

Mother is standing at the edge of the roof with her arms stretched out in front of her. I wave one of the wet diapers in the air as a measure of submission.

"There can only be one mother," she calls, flapping her arms in the air.

I move closer to the house and hold my arms out in front of me. Perhaps I'm not strong enough to catch her, I think, and she'll come crashing through the front lawn. She'll land on the man's mud pies and splatter the clean diapers with her mess.

"You're still the mother," I call.

The Timex ticks on my wrist. I hold my arms out and bend at the knees, waiting for the feel of her in my arms. No matter how hard I try I can't seem to open my eyes. I stand there with my eyes closed waiting for her to jump. She calls my name over and over. Who's to say she won't run away after I've caught her or try to drown herself in the sea? How will I save her when the baby comes? I stand there thinking of these things with my arms outstretched and my eyes closed. I can't bear to see where she might land.

Peggy Shinner

Our Bodies Spoke In Tongues

Peggy Shinner's fiction has appeared in *Western Humanities Review, Another Chicago Magazine*, an anthology titled *Her Face in the Mirror/Jewish Women on Mothers and Daughters*, and other publications. Recently she was nominated for a Pushcart Prize. She lives and teaches in Chicago.

Our Bodies Spoke in Tongues

Do I mean when I say that we had sex last night that we started at the beginning? That we started fifteen years ago? That one of us started with a touch of the hand? That the other responded in kind? That entwined we held on? That we haven't let go? Do I mean when I say that we had sex last night that our bodies touched each other? That we kissed one another? That one of us kissed the mouth, ear, neck of the other? That we lingered on each other's breasts? That we fondled head to toe? Do I mean when I say that we had sex last night that one or both of us made sounds? That one of us reminded the other the window was open, to keep her voice down? That one of us heard someone walk by? That one of us heard talking as someone walked by? That the other stifled her cry? That neither of us made any noise? That all we did was talk? That one of us lavished words upon the other? Love talk? Sex talk? That sometimes we can't get beyond talking? That sometimes we're stifled by words? Do I mean when I say that we had sex last night that I cupped your head in my hands? That you slid your tongue in my mouth? That the inside of your mouth felt like the inside of your vagina? That I took your hand from the inside of my leg because it was too soon? That I ran my foot up and down your thigh? That you breathed hot air over me like a feather? That we rubbed together like matches? That your nipples became erect? That I took your hand again? That I slipped your finger inside me? Do I mean when I say that we had sex last night that we experienced sexual feelings? That we felt sexy? Aroused? Excited? That you touched me in such a way that I responded? That I looked at you with lust? That you felt

85

desire? Desirable? Desired? Do I mean when I say that we had sex last night that I held you while you used your vibrator? That I got aroused while you used your vibrator? That I used my hand while you used your vibrator? That you had an orgasm using your vibrator? That I had an orgasm using my hand? Do I mean when I say that we had sex last night that one or both of us was nervous? That it was humbling? Ordinary? Rejuvenating? Essential? Transformative? Perfunctory? Profound? Do I mean when I say that we had sex last night that you kissed my labia? Licked around my clitoris? Parted my lips with your tongue? Moved your tongue around in a circle? Made me wet? Made me cry out? Made me rise up? Made me press your head against my vulva? Made me come? Made me do the same things to you? Do I mean when I say that we had sex last night that when we had sex last night I was thinking of someone setting our house on fire? That I was thinking that what we were doing was dangerous? That I was wondering if what we were doing, in the state of Illinois, was a criminal offense? That I was wondering at the offense of my thoughts? That I was wondering if the shade was down? That I was wondering if our reflection would show in the window? That I was trying to concentrate on what we were doing? That I thought what if you knew what I was thinking? That I was thinking too much?

Do I say when I say that we had sex last night that it was the first time in two months? The first time since my mother died? The first time in a long time? Do I say when I say that we had sex last night that for the first time in a long time we felt desire? That it was the first time you felt your desire reciprocated? That it was the first time I felt my desire appropriate? That it was the first time we acted on our mutual desire? Do I say when I say that we had sex last night that I was afraid of feeling aroused? That I was afraid of the feelings arousal would arouse? Do I say when I say that we had sex last night that I was afraid I'd forgotten how? That I would touch you in the wrong place? The wrong way? That I would do it incorrectly? I would let you down? Do I say when I say that we had sex last night that you were afraid of being out of control? That you wanted to be in charge because you were afraid to lose control? Do I say when I say that we had sex last night that at first I didn't want to but then I got aroused? That I got aroused in spite of my desire not to? That I didn't want to do it even though I got aroused? Do I say when I say that we had sex last night that afterwards you want to be close? That after we're close I pull away? That when you feel rested, you want more? That when we have more, it's enough?

Do I say when I say that we had sex last night that my mother said it was killing her? That she said I was selfish? That she said she wasn't to blame? Do I say when I say that we had sex last night that my brother said what's the big deal? That it made no difference to him? Do I say when I say that we had sex last night that after reading one of my stories, my father cut out all the sexual references? He cut out the reference every time it appeared? Do I say when I say that we had sex last night that your parents never say anything? They never utter a word? Do I say when I say that we had sex last night that people often ask if we're sisters? They even ask if we're twins? Some say it's the glasses? Others the hair? Do I say when I say that we had sex last night that we danced slow at my brother's wedding? That we danced cheek to cheek, arm in arm? Do I say when I say that we had sex last night that we own a house in joint tenancy? That together we purchased a car? Do I say when I say that we had sex last night that you are my sole beneficiary? That I've left you everything I've got?

Meaning when I say that we had sex last night that first we read erotica in bed, remarking how poorly it was written, taking turns reading it out loud, wondering what possessed C. to buy it because we would never spend money on such trash? Meaning that while we read erotica in bed last night we couldn't stop laughing, every once in a while kissing, that next we read another story, turning the pages, kissing some more, that soon the book fell between the covers and our tongues skimmed each other's mouths, that you rolled on top of me and I wrapped my legs around you, that the covers got all tangled and the book landed on the floor; that you got your just desserts, that this was my comeuppance? Meaning when I say that we had sex last night that afterwards we ate, that you craved pound cake, that you had a craving for a Sara Lee pound cake with strawberries, that we ate the pound cake in bed, scooping it up with our fingers, that afterwards I had a taste for a sandwich, a hot pastrami sandwich, that it was ten o'clock when we drove to The Bagel for a sandwich, that first we ate chopped egg and onions, spreading it on fresh challah, that next I ordered hot pastrami on an onion roll and to drink a chocolate phosphate and you ordered potato soup? Meaning when I say that we had sex last night that I stroked your butt lightly with my fingers, kneaded it with the palms of my hands, that I felt your muscles contracting, relaxing, that I rubbed my cheeks against your cheeks, that I spread your well-shaped cheeks apart, separating the folds of your vulva, moving my tongue from the dampness of your labia to the dampness of your anus, moving it back and forth in a circular motion, moving you back and forth? Meaning when I say that we had sex last night that you were on the tip of my tongue, that I said your name, each and every letter, nuance, meaning defining our definitions, articulating our feelings, that our bodies embodied our feelings, they spoke in tongues, in words, in multiple meanings, that what we were doing had meaning, linguistically, semantically, syntactically, that using our hands, our mouths, our ears, our eyes, our hearts, our minds, our breasts, our thighs, our clits, our vulvas, our voices we expressed our selves, by commission, by omission, deliberately, intentionally, our meanings were complex, our actions complicated, that what was on the tip of my tongue was just the tip of the iceberg, that what my fingertips conveyed just scratched the surface.

Lily James

Up There

Lily James recently completed her MA in the Program for Writers at the University of Illinois at Chicago. She is the founder and editor of *Big Girl Press*, is the lead singer in a rock band called *Stiff Kitty*, and owns a large hound dog.

Up There

His nose and his dick are both hard, and Paul is on the roof on top of the skylight looking down. With his face pressing down and his dick straight, the nose and dick are pushing up on his head and hips, but not uncomfortably. His arms and legs are stretched out as far as they'll go, and now his stomach is flat because the window is arched up toward him and shapes his body. In this light you can tell he's not tan except for around his wrists and his face. He's about forty-five. When his eyelashes brush on the window it makes him shiver and he doesn't like it, you see that, but he has to keep his eyes open and looking, so he can see down below where there are things going on he has to watch. You see him try to shift around and is it that his skin is stuck with some kind of glue or is gravity so much that he can't lift his head away? His hair seems limp with the snow falling in it, and too long for how curly it is. When he tries to lift his head up to blink the hair pulls down around the glass and sticks to it. His fingers uncurl, curl, his toes clench in rhythm or he just kind of presses down with his hips on what's up there.

In a room below are four men who can't get it up at all. The shrink's office has some electrical wires falling in the ceiling from under one plaster looking styrofoam tile in the corner. The light doesn't quite get back there. One of the men looks up at these wires, while the others sit in their chairs and wait for the shrink to come in. She wears neutral colors for the same reason that the room's panelling isn't too dark, but it still depresses some patients, or it calms them. When she comes in she acts like she doesn't know one of them is missing, but the short one with dark hair and a moustache points it out.

"Where's Paul?" he asks with a smirk.

"Sidney, Paul is not coming back," she answers, putting her notebook under her folding chair. She sits in on the circle, but five isn't enough to make it a real circle. Six would be enough.

One of the men, the one in the nicest suit, leans forward to take his back off the folding chair, and rests his elbows on his knees. He seems calm enough, but the one who looks the least nervous is also the youngest, wearing jeans and a burgundy silk shirt. His hair is very short and he has blue color contacts. The last one is still staring at the ceiling, now at the skylight. He has short boots on that could be riding boots, and grey pants that could be for work, or for warmth. Outside the snow is pretty bad.

"Probably got laid," Sidney says. Sidney also wears a suit but his body isn't made for that, so it bunches at his waist. Todd's body is made for nice suits. Todd's fingers cross and uncross and he has a pretty bone structure in his face.

"Do you think that would make you stop coming here, if you had sex one time?" asks the shrink, not of Sidney but of whoever.

"Hell yeah," says the youngest one, whose mouth moves nastily when he talks, "It'd take me about a minute to figure that one out."

"It was probably that woman he was talking about last week. Geneva. She probably had sex with him," offers Todd, not looking up.

"If I had a woman..." begins the younger one, Joe.

"If you had my wife you'd know that a woman's not the first thing you want."

"Have you been able to get an erection this week, or have you tried?" asks the shrink, not directing it at anyone certain.

"Christ," mutters Rick at the ceiling.

"I'll tell you at home with my wife I don't get a moment to myself, even if I could get it up for a wank, you know what I mean?" Sidney raises his eyebrows several times at the group.

"Yeah, I got an erection, right in the middle of the stupid

night," says Joe. His silk shirt is buttoned open enough to see a downy bit of fuzz on his dark chest. He has always talked about high school and standing in front of the class with a 'big-ass woody', as if it had been great. Todd has talked about dating women who ask too much, or else they expect too much, or they know too much. Sidney says his wife coddles him, and he always wonders to the group if he forgot how to have sex, like maybe if he could just remember the proper order of steps? Rick doesn't talk about anything and nobody can find out who made him come to this therapy. Nobody knows.

"You know," the shrink starts in, "Paul was always talking about how impotence of this sort, of the sort you have, was sure to be caused by a strictly physical problem. Perhaps he found out that he was dealing with a psychological issue after all."

"With a woman like Geneva, it doesn't make a hell of a lot of difference, now does it?" Joe laughs, pulling his mouth down, and his big lips down.

"How would you know?" Sidney asks.

"I saw her, you know, hello, she was a babe of paradise."

"Big girl or little?"

Geneva paints houses not with big heavy strokes but little short ones up and down even if the panelling runs side to side— she'll fix it up later—Geneva wears painting overalls because she's so thin or because she can get them ruined with paint *God damn it* there goes another glob of peach paint down on the petunias and them striped red and white—it'll look awful—she always eats her lunch on the ladder because why go down but then sometimes she bumps the paint can with her butt and spills it the window opens beside her and there's a head of an old woman telling her *don't mind the flowers* but in a very sarcastic way so she says *okay* as if she didn't notice the sarcasm and tries to look down sideways to see how much paint actually got down there—and it's a lot—so she does try to appear apologetic but the old woman is raising one eyebrow and maybe she's funny—maybe she's okay—Geneva half smiles as an experiment and the old woman grabs her arm as if she were about to fall and laughs hysterically she's not an old woman with red rimmed eyes or messy lips with caked up lipstick in fact no makeup at all and pretty nice eyes *I'm almost done eating* says Geneva maybe to make the woman feel bad about razzing her because she knows old people don't like thin young girls not to eat and the woman props her elbows in the window and props up her chin and squints in the sun which has made Geneva all blonde and brown.

"Big girl," continues Joe, "but not too big on the tits or butt. She doesn't need them believe me."

"Is that the girl who picked him up from the bar last week?" asks Todd.

"Yeah, after... thing. Did you see her?"

"She's great. She's like a model, if they didn't want models to be such freaks. You remember Christie Brinkley? Now there."

They just can't go ahead and say Hold me back, or Easy Willie, so nobody says anything to agree or disagree. In the bar later maybe they will bring this point up again, and make some comments.

"Is that what she looked like," asks Sidney. "Hey if my wife looked like that I'd have no problems. I mean none. You know what I'm saying?"

Joe doesn't have a girlfriend and neither does Todd. Rick has an ex-wife.

"If I had Geneva for a girlfriend... She probably sucked his dick, or something. If I had a face like that in my crotch—"

The shrink has told them to forget she is there, and sometimes they do.

"What's it got to do with her face," says Rick, "When it's not the face that counts."

He has a little bit of beard and a crisp white shirt tucked into those heavy pants. His hands are tough, not puffy like Sidney's or smooth like Todd's. Joe's hands are small and have hair on them in tufts.

"Would you be happy with a perfect woman?" the shrink sits up straight in her chair with her legs crossed all the time, and never switches legs.

"Hell yes," Joe jumps in, "I'd be so happy then, perfectly happy."

"This is different from some of the things that you've said in other sessions," the shrink smiles a small smile without crinkling her eyes, "I wonder if you are feeling betrayed because Paul isn't here anymore and because he feels he no longer has a problem with sex."

"I'm just glad somebody's getting it," says Sidney.

"I don't feel betrayed," says Todd.

"Gee," says Rick, "I guess we all could be getting it, if we could fucking take it."

The shrink nods at Rick as if she wants them to get back on track like before Paul left and got better but he's done talking again.

"Listen," says Todd, "This just goes a long way to prove that if you had the right woman, there wouldn't be a problem. She probably doesn't make him undress in front of her, and she probably doesn't make him turn the lights out until he's ready and she probably says 'Paul, Paul' instead of 'God, God'."

"She probably does."

Maybe the rules in this city are that the bus driver gets to have sex with the very last person on the bus if it is a woman and the bus driver is a man so Geneva gets off the bus one stop early all the time and she would rather take the van everywhere that she drives at work but it's not her van and anyway she can't parallel park—not very well—so what would she do with it she is wearing black pants because she is ovulating and it leaves a spot on her panties every time which smells like the balls of whoever she sucked off last so that's why she keeps going back to her ex-boyfriend because she doesn't want her pussy smelling like some stranger the man at the corner store gives her extra lemon in her iced tea that she is buying and she says *thanks* and he doesn't let on like he knows she knows— who's looking over his shoulder—by the time she gets home her iced tea is only half gone and she puts it in the refrigerator for later where it can get tasting like the wax on the outside of the paper cup—does it seep through there—and she calls up the guy from the club which the napkin says Paul and then the number.

"What I want to know is," says Sidney with one finger held up in the air for silence, "Who here has ever gotten a real blow job, a good one, like Geneva gives?"

The shrink's eyes don't change but she looks at Rick.

"I think the kind Geneva gives is pretty rare. She uses all kinds of tricks," says Todd, finally leaning back against his chair.

"When Geneva gives head she uses just enough teeth that you know they're there."

"And dangles her boobs down there."

"And she doesn't let you come right away."

Joe laughs and shows he has a good smile.

"Maybe she doesn't let you come for a long time," he says, "until you think you never will."

His tone has taken on a slow and mysterious tone but relaxed like telling stories around a fire at night, when you have everyone's attention. His skin is dark and smooth. He is the only one in the room without a few wrinkles.

"Now Todd here," he says, "Can make her let him come when he's ready. He might use his hand or he might not, but he's going to come when he's ready."

The men chuckle a little, and don't take offense. Todd doesn't appear to feel offended at all in fact he holds up his hand and motions them to wait as if he has a better one.

"When she goes down on me," he says, "I've got my hand on the back of her head. But I don't push," he glances around for effect, "I just feel her hair."

"Her blond hair."

"And the beauty of it is that I don't even think she realizes I could be pushing. I don't think it enters her mind."

The shrink shifts but doesn't uncross her legs. The men are accustomed to the way she looks at her watch sideways. It's not really meant to be that subtle. After a long pause the men realize that Joe has an erection.

She can taste what he has been drinking and it's good when he pulls her around the corner to try out her kissing at the same club they were at before, she can taste what he has been drinking and it tastes different and he's not making any noise, feeling her up, and his dick isn't hard thank god for her friend that came with her—to meet him here—and is waiting with the car around front for her to get done with him so this leaves it much less complicated if he doesn't even want her but why is he kissing her still and pushing down the back of her top which is a sleeveless black slutty thing—sweat on his fingers—there goes his hand again up in her hair well okay if it gets a little messy now but really she is strong and could stop him *nice tan* he says finally pulling away to look at her with her t-shirt line around her arm and she thinks is this humiliating or should I grab his limp dick and that would show him *I could suck this until it comes off in my mouth* she says for no reason but that he's still looking at her arms and he says *You have my number* — inching back away from her—and she pulls him back and bites his lips and now feels a little rise in his zipper.

"Joe, you seem to have become aroused," says the shrink.

Joe pinches his knees together and no one will look at him. His face is pinched up around the cheekbones like the erection hurts him, or like it's making his balls uncomfortable and twisted in his underwear. He looks like he wants to adjust his pants, but his hands are down by his knees.

"It would be good," she goes on, "If you could talk about what made you feel stimulated. Maybe you —"

"Hey," Sidney smiles broadly and tilts his head as if to show he understands, "Why not? He's a boy and he's thinking about a girl. He's a boy."

"Have you ever had an erection in public, Sidney?" asks the shrink.

"Me? No."

"I think," Todd's eyes don't swing around toward Joe, but he talks to Joe anyway, "Maybe you feel okay here, but when you get to where someone's all over you, you know you're going to have to make something happen."

"I think that's a good observation, Todd," says the shrink, "Could you go on? What do you mean by safe, safe from what?"

Joe stands up and is walking out of the room, and then they all look around.

"You think he's slapping off?" asked Sidney quickly.

"Hey, it's not like he's making a finger painting. You're not going to hang it on the fucking refrigerator."

Everyone looks at Rick and even the shrink seems surprised. Rick's legs are spread apart, obviously he's not hard, and his pants are loose in the hips. He has small hips, but he has big shoulders.

"That's sick, is all I can say," he says, "That guy is sick."

"Just because he got a hard on?" asks Todd quietly.

"That's not what happened. He didn't get hard for a woman."

"Geneva has a strange effect on men, you don't understand."

Rick raises one side of his lip, "When I had Geneva she didn't make me strange. She didn't make me act like a fool."

Sidney pushes his chin down into his neck, incredulous.

"What'd you do to her then?"

"I'll tell you," says Rick, sitting up straight. His light brown eyes are getting them one by one so they won't look away. "I met her at a hotel restaurant. She came in a dress, but tight all the way down to her feet and green. But there was a slit up the side. And I didn't even have to say anything. There were four buttons up at her neck and they just came undone, she took that off and underneath that was a — what looked like all messed up skin and bruises. Big bruises up here on her shoulders and fucked up down at her hips like somebody cut her, but she was smiling, and put her finger in her ear and started peeling an edge. She scratched up an edge and peeled it down, and it unwrapped over her nose and her face, down, left it so clean, cleaner than you could ever wash it. She had to peel in a few pieces, like four, but then it was all off and she had no hair and no bruises and no dirt."

Todd pulls his jacket around and buttons it, but can't sit down like that. He unbuttons it. Sidney has his face in a shocked expression and the shrink is placidly tracing the leg of her folding chair with one finger.

"When you had sex with Geneva," she says slowly, "were you able to sustain an erection?"

Rick sucks on the inside of his bottom lip and widens his eyes. He nods.

"Did you become aroused after the bruises came off?" asks the shrink.

"Then I —"

"Did you stop there or did you go on and have sex with her?"

"With Geneva?"

"That's right."

"I had sex with her."

"He did not," Sidney jumps in, "He got right up to her and his dick went like a wet spaghetti noodle."

"Hey," says Todd, "Easy there."

The toilet flushes in the bathroom next to them but since Joe doesn't immediately come back in, Sidney says, "He must have used the one down the hall. Or downstairs."

"He probably left," says Todd.

"Are you tired?" asks the shrink, "We're just about out of time."

You see that Paul's skin will be dried out from this weather, and he is watching the men go out different doors as if he is sad to see it is over with. The snow blows around him and catches on him then blows away or makes drifts in the crevices, clinging piles around the hair. He shifts the weight with great effort off of his penis and onto one hipbone, but it quickly becomes too difficult to keep his other hipbone up so he drops back down. Inch by inch he creeps his right hand toward his face to scratch his eye, and then creeps it back out so it is extended again. Todd and the shrink are talking about something, but you see Paul is not interested in that conversation, his eyes are on Joe who has come back in the room to get his coat. Paul's forehead is so cold it must send aching pain into his head, that brittle solid cold pain. You see him close his eyes for a second after Joe leaves and then look back at Todd and the shrink. He squints his eyes from the wind and then starts creeping his hand back up again to push the hair out of his face so he can see.

She can see that the paint isn't mixed enough and stirs it with her wooden flat stick and it still has swirls of unmixed paint it's not a great brand either—today is not so sunny—the old woman has a friend over at her house Geneva can see who has thin hips and a boy about twelve who comes to the window *Can I help with that* he asks *No* says Geneva *if you fell off this ladder your grandma'd be mad at me* the boy looks down to the ground from inside the house—bending his neck over—and Geneva shifts on the ladder to show how creaky it is she's pretty high and the boy looking out is impressed and sits down so he can look out the window—the back of the house—the old woman's dog is tired on the back porch the dog has his legs around his food dish and is asleep in it but it's empty when Geneva looks down she likes the kind of scared feeling because she has both hands wrapped around the ladder whenever she looks down and she never extends it until the doubled up part is shorter than the single part—you can die—she never wants to shock anyone by falling who might be in the house at the time and anyway she used to stretch a tightrope across trees about ten feet up for the neighborhood kids when she was young and the only one who would stand up there.

Thalia Field

$$A \therefore I$$

Thalia Field has recently completed an NEA commissioned opera, *The Pompeii Exhibit,* with composer Toshiro Saruya. An excerpt of a longer work-in-progress was published in the spring 1995 issue of *Conjunctions.*

A ∴ I

I occupy this comfortable chair in your office and you stare at me. We are not speaking to one another, so you've called this uncomfortable time *silence*.

A cat wanders around your legs.

I rushed here and made it on time to the door, stood outside and turned up late. Now I find it funny you should have produced this thoughtful word *silence*. A cat falls from a bookshelf and lands on its spleen.

A cat gathers itself up to jump. A pleasure to watch. A relief to see a creature inhabiting itself comfortably. I bask in the waves of unlit sound that fill my mouth.

I have heard that staring is a predator's first weapon.

A big bang, a spot, one first cell, a tiny clue, a kernel of truth, an unrevealed fact that puts all of me in perspective—Your job is to espy and co-author that spot. Across the horizon the searchlight seems sourceless and harder to deflect.

I think I'll keep pointing out the cat. That

specific cat, I don't know it's name. How easily it slips from the room.

A foghorn intrudes and the lighthouse beam cuts through a marsh. The probing light keeps night ships wary of land—aware of land as an obstacle or a destination.

I am not speaking to you but if you could get beyond that, there is much to celebrate. Minutes have passed. Ten kicks to the pendulum to compensate for the effects of air resistance.

An eye grows accustomed and then shapes are visible in a dark room though it's been said that the shapes *emerge*. A basket of plastic flowers looks beautiful on your desk.

I count on the fact that in another thirty minutes our session will end and I'll walk back onto a street where nobody is speaking to me and yet I would never call it *silent*.

A girl strolls along a bustling Saturday market, walking alone from fence to fence, around the backs of benches, wandering without stalling.

I see another basket, empty of plastic flowers, where plastic flowers may not belong.

A job, what a job—yours—to connect so many carelessly scattered spots. The spread of seeds, the search for new stars. The whole entanglement of sowing and harvest is utterly for the birds—which is why the birds are such menaces to the farmers. And big scarecrows guard the broken earth. And the bats come out at night to suck the fruit.

I think if I spoke now you'd devour the sounds and still feel unsatisfied. People only stop eating when they've swallowed enough. I find myself staring at my hands, turning a ring around my finger.

A girl in your book is never alone. So I will be the third person here. A girl in an open-air market speaks to no one, as she was taught to do by a protective parent, or by experience. And so she is silent, and so you'd say we are identical. Eden is impossible to find on a map and yet people point to it as the first place, the justifiable cause of where we are today.

I won't pick up the looks you flick onto the rug between us. This is the "most silent you've ever seen me", and your seeing has become more incisive since you've made a career of it. *How many times do you see her? Oh, I see her twice a week.*

A moth saw a flame and thought what it saw was its heart and it said "what is my heart doing over there, away from me?" And believing that it could not be whole without an organ it had never even used, the moth dove toward it, hoping to reabsorb it in open surgery, but instead there was a sound as empty as a lit match skipped on a surface of water, and in an instant the heart that had stood away from the moth became the central unimagined ecstasy the moth couldn't live without.

I fear there is no such thing as being naked in language.

A hood has practical use and histories of concealment. A veil. The eyelid is a very sensual place to be kissed. A kiss here, no matter how delicate, shocks the eyeball underneath which doesn't yet think of itself as a physical sphere able to be touched. And the brain doesn't know how this touch feels, there is no word for it. A hood hides a spot in every culture. In some the concealing is worshipped, in some destroyed—and you can't tell which—yet you want desperately to find it, to feel it, to finger it.

I may writhe in a pleasure that I didn't know I had, that you can show me, that is really your pleasure.

A hand skims back and forth causing small ripples as if the ocean were merely sink water.

I won't emerge. The Polaroid camera is empty of film: the feeling you have when you discover that all those carefully framed candids are lost without permission: *we would have lived life differently had we only known the damn thing was empty!* A girl is approached by a man in the market. He will ask her if she's lost, not where she's going.

A cat pushes his way into the room, we both look. He rubs against the couch, and then first my knees and then yours, joining us with his attention. The silence becomes louder.

I try and forget how tightly sealed the window is as I focus on the street scene through it—as I focus on breathing and not on the air in my lungs. I will not become transparent.

A girl searches an open-air market for something to buy with the change in her pocket.

Her slow appraisals take on the rhythm of water spilling across a table top, growing as vastly clear as sunlight on a blank wall. A stranger in the room would call this silence *full*.

I'm going to ask the question at the end of our time, as your hand reaches for the door, "Is that cat alive or dead?

A hat flies up and a girl loses it in the blinding hole, the sun. It spills on the concrete and she steps off the sidewalk to pick it up, looking to see if anyone saw her. An amateur astronomer prays at the base of his telescope as the glow from a fifteen million year old supernova reaches him, steadily brightening.

I feel my cheeks burn as if they might peel off my face and fly toward the window, striking against it, a terrifying wet bird.

A girl sniffs the gyros from a full block away, remembering the salty oil and the soft wings of meat, desiring them as she approaches the colorful stands of banners. A girl finds her way through a market, searching for a way to spend her money. She thought she would buy a scarf but now she's hungry.

I guess you could say I've brought this situation on myself: sitting here like paying for a parking space when I don't own a car. We don't spend money on words when we put them to waste, so why spend it on the choice not to use them?

A network TV movie languishing unmade, you'd say.
I could sell the rights if I could simply tell the

story. You can't say I haven't complied when I could, throwing you some real doozies to mull over in your fascinating way. And the smell of relief on your breath when I do toss up some details! I try to use the normal kind I have spent a lifetime stealing from strangers; knocking them on the heads and emptying their stories into velvet sacks to pull back before you, leaving a pile of glittering stones, you see them as jewels—what you believe is the valuable ore of my deepest soul visible across a table. They sparkle in your eyes and you tackle them efficiently and with style. Suddenly crime seems to pay. So that you can lean back and uncross your legs, looking as relaxed as you'd like me to be.

"A" sounds like "I" when spoken.

I sort of wish you'd tap that pencil. But that sort of gesture, with or without reason, has been labeled unprofessional.

A third ring.

I stare at you. The phone rings a forth time and the answering machine sucks the sound into its plastic body where on turning tape a voice discharges.

A voice is calling out to you.

I know you want to press the blinking light, lean in, soak up the wet sweet words. However, owing to your professionalism, you can only shoot glances at the clock.

A strategy has prevailed as in all battles; the power of suggestion.

"So how was your week-end, after all?"

Oh I know what you mean with that *after all*. There's the story you want—and then there's that pleasure driving too fast that in speaking would slow way down and vanish, the motion rolling to a stop with the friction if I would try to describe what happened.

A spot like that can't be looked into. A place on the map, a motel for fossils that slip out at night and skulk along the cooled sidewalks, leaning back flat against painted wood, familiar patterns of bones casting Sanskrit shadows.

I know that between any two people is the potential to give birth to the world. It must have begun with two just like us, sitting in comfortable chairs, not speaking. Would that epic infant look like me or you? The fantasy of having my mother's baby fills my throat. If this is transference, am I allowed to ask you to remove your shirt?

A payment of money for this is ridiculous.

I *surveyed the ceiling of my prison...It was the painted figure of Time as he is commonly represented, save that, in lieu of a scythe, he held what, at a casual glance, I supposed to be the picture of a pendulum.* You keep twisting the watch around your wrist as though time might gain momentum. You need to throw me something. A swath of speech that you can see, but which, falling covers more.

"You took care of yourself I hope."

A cat like yours is a Schrodinger's cat, sealed up in an office where someone's disintegration provides a 50-50 chance of its death. *Take care of her*, says the mobster to the hitman, winking verbally. At the end of the hour the lip will be lifted to see the results.

I've never seen you this way. Darkness and a hushed room are alike when you walk into them. A night sky and a silent God have a lot in common.

An irresponsible look brews in your eyes.

I may repeat stories about *a girl* in so many different forms you think you're encountering a life. Maybe you think it's my life? Always assume that nothing relates. A girl, the invention of plastic, amateur cosmologists, "I", "you", pieces of paper, your chair, it's just a combination that continues until a stopping place is reached and the time is up, frame blasted, and then it continues despite us. The cat sits alive, dead or whatever it is just inside the door licking its folded paw.

A girl once went to confession and said, *I have never spoken truthfully about myself*, to a priest whose eyes widened as he nodded in that fascinating way.
I know you need me to start speaking up before I become dangerous.

A parade of lives passes outside the window, sealed out. Silent, and yet you don't seem as concerned about them.

I lean forward and think we shouldn't see each other any more. I might say I spent the weekend idling outside a motel in a northern town. You would ask me why did I come back. I would ask why I was idling. Why didn't I forever. I found an open place and I watched it come into view. A raw motel. A car parked suddenly. A place of clothing. An entrance. If I named my sins they would become obligations. On my back finally opened sideways on a brown bedspread I thought pleasantly of nothing while I gave pleasure with my tongue.

A billboard comes down piece by piece. A wall, a line, a galaxy or the flesh of our heads stands between us. What makes you think this space between us is empty? Where you see a barrier, there is a place of opportunity.

I do flatter you with a look now and then, which you grab up eagerly like undeserved flowers. In one flower you could hear a thousand words, but you can't read minds, you've often said, trying to keep my gaze from falling back to the window, which of course I let it do.

A room in which walls, ceiling and floor are totally bare behaves to sound in the same way as it would to light if it were lined with mirrors. When two people communicate their brains begin to mirror each other and the boundaries between them dissolve.

I wonder what is it about darkness that makes us think we can't move safely through it. Something about bumping into things with our bodies first. That the touch might be painful, erotic, before we understand it.

A pair of cats rushes entangled in, a live cat and a dead cat screeching and hissing, baring excruciating flashes of claw. This display brings you to your feet and you chase them away.

I cautiously moved forward, with my arms extended, and my eyes straining from their sockets, in the hope of catching some faint ray of light. I have never lied in so many words.

A buttonhole can never be enough. My fingers curl back to find it. I could slip in a plastic flower or a finger.

I drove through fog on my way north and the headlights made even the tiniest particles of air blaze. I could see best without any beams on at all.

A girl laughed out loud leaving the confession booth where behind the wooden panel the priest had grown angrier and angrier, shaking the whole box with outrage as minutes passed and the girl would neither speak nor leave. *Make her do one or the other*, he prayed.

A billboard rises in the dusty sunset saying something about buying or driving a new car. On the sign I see myself walking into a hardware store for cigarettes and then on the way out I glance up at the billboard and see I'm having a good smoke.

I think *window* several times. In the mind words are heard bone-dry, without the benefit of breath. Silence is the thread of the buttonhole, what holds the button, what I lick to get through the needle.

At first your questions—like flashlights toward Orion—vanished into the paradox of the dark night sky: an infinite universe filled infinitely with stars should make any line of sight eventually hit a star in the sky, strike a word, a memory. This being so, and there being infinite lines of sight, why is the night sky dark and not a screen of burning light?

Edgar Allen Poe thought about this and concluded that time was on his side. The farther into space he looked the further back in time he saw—back to where stories first formed in fiery spit and crashing density—and he realized that even if he couldn't travel the past, he could simply wait and it would come to him. "The only mode, therefore...in which we could comprehend the voids which our telescopes find in innumerable directions, would be by supposing the distance of the invisible background so immense that no ray from it has yet been able to reach us at all."

And the thing I'm counting on is that time is on my side too, that I can sit here for long enough for you to run that clock down and admit a certain defeat with the envelope I'll hand you with the fee for our time together. In many ways, we are as gothic as the thick illogical spaces between the stars, between good ideas, between motel rooms. For different reasons, we may both be right: I am making myself crazy.

A car pulls up outside your building and begins honking.

I traveled alone in a real metal vehicle, the touch of the vinyl, the invitation of familiar

113

music to a foot, a certain weight collecting, bearing down on a pedal accelerating. The sky was brewing a darker drink as I idled outside the motor lodge.

A girl loses her change purse and tries to retrace where she's been, the booths in the market, the paths between strangers. Markets made from unsuitable materials sway in the steady breeze, half-crooked nails pulling from the soft wood, the tarp across the top flies off, the crafts on display scoot along the sidewalks. So much for the open-air, for the kinds of structures people build in temporary places. Before she can return to it, it is coming undone.

I know you are a progeny of Poe and that I, too formless to have a counter theory to his, stubbornly occupy a losing position. For you have faith that at the horizon of what you can see lies *the creation*, awaiting revelation, emerging for your inspection. The farther light travels, the harder the words come, the more they reflect the original state of things. Numerous but feeble rays whispering the inchoate message of the big bang. Admit it, in my silence you think you see the possibility of everything there is to know about me. A dictionary left on this leather chair when I go would serve you equally in conjuring me up. I refer to this kind of realization when I offer you the words,

"I think I'm leaving here."

A better Poe might have said something about the expanding universe that moves away from itself at all times, that perhaps has no center, that at all points is moving in many directions at once so the future and the past are just fences to bump against as we feel for a shape in the wild openness.

I counted the rushing vibrations of the steel! Inch by inch, line by line—

A false distinction lies between music and a garbageman pulling cans from the pavement.

I know in the city the sky at night isn't dark at all—and that's one reason we may never have been possible. When the lights were out and I lay across the brown bedspread, the face that leaned down and touched mine was as empty as a window.

"Talk to me about it."

A whole nest of starving possibilities fall between us and yet you reach in and pull out only the easiest to save. I understand why you look at me the way you do, a boarded up window with a window painted on it: a vow of understanding is the most irrational contract there is.

I watch the cat which is now a messy melange of live and dead cats.

A girl runs through the market with the scarf she stole as the booths collapsed and she holds its softly hemmed edges between her fingers. When she reaches an alley where nobody can see her she runs hands out to the full length of the fabric, folding it around her head.

I feel a constriction in my chest. What can I do to ask you to open the window?

A girl travels in the city unrecognized. Her age and her face are covered in soft blue printed cotton. She was happy when I first saw her, she is even happier now.

I am afraid to use those words about the window. Their usage may lead them to execution, and I don't mean completion of action.

A girl smokes, leaning against a pier and smiling at someone beyond the blue-sky frame of the billboard. My desire is to know her desire.

I am really the criminal you won't say I am. In instance after instance, I kill you. And each procession I hear of myself is a funeral. The hill is muddy, silence surrounds your coffin and because you are dead, even the patter of the dirt as it touches you is like affection you can't feel. Too bad you have to die in here. Some of me is very sorry and whistles to disrupt the killing spree. Some of me wants to torture you because you make it so easy. Some of me is the guard on duty who looks blithely the other way and later denies the whole affair. I am all the murderers who served their silence up cold; for a heading home of thoughts that needed to wander. Can you tell I'm looking at you now—

A vacuum of agreement is between us.

I reach across the two feet of space and lift the window without asking. I open windows frequently. There is no reverberation to my act as I let the impatient rustle of traffic into what you persist in seeing as a silent room.

A sound made in the open air travels away, and for the most part doesn't return.

I hear the street like a reprieve. It doesn't know it but it screams my release, not from any real silence, but from the biting indiscretion of your frown. I am so aware of all the noise outside I can barely look at you. And how is it that you don't know my mind is as loud as your staring at my hands, now that they are refusing to fidget as they have in the past. In the stillness of my hands you suddenly think you hear something.

A star once discovered is given a name. New words come into the language as technology changes, as people change. Still, there are light waves you do not see which go into your mind undetected. There are sounds that flow up through your feet from where I've pushed the earth and it's pushed you back.

I pay you money so that we may share this kind of history.

A car runs smoothly when the teeth of one gear enter and leave the spaces of another. The better made the wheels, the more silently they turn.

I am still unable to achieve the silence you accuse me of. The murderer's father appears more guilty than his son when asked about their Sunday dinners or why he suspected nothing.

A girl realizes that someone is staring at her.

Into the fisheye of a telescope on a planet as blue and distant as a pleasant smell, she thumbs her nose and pull her face into a smile.

I can't think of a more sublime torture than a subpoena.

A girl is racing now, away from something she thinks is following her. A girl dashed past me on the way in here, and I stood for several minutes outside your door, hoping to eventually emerge as her, or at least running that quickly.

I know a moment before it happens that our time is suddenly over.

"Oh, well!"

A girlish cry as the red digits jump to your eyes like a cat to your lap and you act startled and raise yourself from the chair, half-smiling. Nervously you indicate the clock, your watch, the door, even the answering machine as though you fear I might linger eternally. You want me to see that everything in the room has conspired to elapse. Yet that is all I ever wanted. That, and this intimate look.

mary hope whitehead lee

story

mary hope whitehead lee works and teaches in Oakland, CA, in a community where the barrio, the hood and the urban res collide and merge with fragments of Asia. Her work has been published in numerous small press publications, and in *Essence* magazine, *Callaloo*, and the award-winning anthology *This Bridge Called My Back: Writing By Radical Women of Color*. She has just recently completed an illustrated biography-in-poems inspired by the life and work of Mexican painter Frida Kahlo.

story

nursin
without a body it seem
nursin

nursin i look down at the head   without a body it seem   face
mouth lips that suckle at one of my always seem to be too sore
nipple and i wants to take this new new baby head tween my
labor large rough workin hands and crush this little fleshy fat
skull into nothinness

nothinness

cant love this child dont care for this child dont want to aint
no one have the power to change the way i feels

the power

felt exactly the same way at the age of nine when i was made
to look after childrens and babies of peoples that works my
mama

work
my mama
work

at the age of nine

she would never not never have wish this work on me just like she never wish to be taken whenever they please by husbands and brothers relations and neighbors friends they say of the womens and mens she labors under

labor
she
labor

hate mindin other peoples childrens and i been all the way all the time uncarin   like this time when that girlchild anne got herself all caught up in some tree that didnt want her up in itself no way and she cry out to me for help i just sits here and she screamin and all starts to gettin on my nerves so i walks up under that tree and tell her—jump

jump

jump i say ima catch you i say   she believe me and she come tumblin down outta that tree too not feet first but head first head first i step aside   tell annies her name anne too mother that her girlbaby fall hit ground fore i can reach her

step aside

remember too the boybabyson of one of them peoples useta works my mama   hate to change it dirty cloths hate the sight of the thing in the crotch of it legs want to pull it off it body just the same way i wants to pull the same thing offa them bodies of all them mens that takes my mama makes my mama do what I knows she hate

i know

she hate that i gots no place else to sleep but in the same room in the same bed with her shame that she cant send me outside while they uses her cause she cant always send me to lena and mama fraid somebody walkin by in the night might take me too hate that she might have to use them herbs again make her so sick cause she need them to root out the thing them mens leave in her body some time   she hate the takin   hate the way they looks at me too like they do when they done finish somehow someway they know they know she would kill   she would   so they just looks

like they do

i know these things cause i hear mama say them all these things and more to lena

lena

lena mama woman friend she give her heart to whenever everytime she can

everytime

i sees them together and what pass between them be the thing i want i done always want still be wantin for myself for me since the first time i done seen it were possible

it be possible

they touch they whisper they laugh they cry out loud they spill forth they soul into each other eye and they aint never seems to fill each other up   bes a sweet need they has for each other

a sweet need
i needs for me
a sweet need

aint no sweet need this sucklin thing at my breast   this child it mother too busy to nurse forcin on me the thing she find unladylike she say beneath her she say not knowin i know she say it   dont want this woman leavins not the leavins of nobody who say i must do gotta do they work cause it demean them have to do it they say

demeanin

123

so it be too too easy for me to see just how soft be this brand new baby skull how it got a soft spot like a hole in the roof of it head that hold it child brain

oh
i was
pregnant
once

i was once and i hate it—being pregnant the thing growin inside me a hungry thing eatin out my soul makin me sick cept when i be sound asleep takin my life for its own use cant keep it no not and keep me too no mama lena both is gone from me now so i carries it to term smother it tell anybody who ask it stillborn nobody seem to care much bury it under the stoop of this old shack so i have milk now is how i come to wet nursin bes my prison

no more
prison
no more

this snufflin small bundle of white babyness seem bout satisfied drift off into sleep now not knowin this it last feedin tiny little head begin to lollin bout on it neck so i brings it baby yellow headed white face tween my two too pain full dark brown breasts and hold it gainst me til it lungs cease pumpin air

cease

Lisa Natalie Pearson

Stage Fright

Lisa Natalie Pearson received her MFA in fiction from the University of Oregon and now lives in Portland. She has worked in theater in Chicago, New York, Seattle, and Europe. Her current project is a novel titled *BABEL*, set in the sexual borderlands of Berlin. In addition to fiction, she writes performance texts, and, when the urge arises, performs them.

Stage Fright

I watched their television because I didn't have one. It was almost always on: a blue cycloptic giant. Their apartment is just across a narrow one-way side street from mine. We are three stories high and the width of two bedsheets apart. There are metal pins and rings twisted into the cracked mortar, rusted pulleys to tether the laundry lines between our buildings. Reminders of arias sung from windowsills, of neighborhood dramas. There's too much smog, dust, and car exhaust now to hang clothes outside. I use the coin-operated washer and dryer in the basement.

Every evening it began around seven o'clock when the sun had just slipped below the rooftops. I sat in my armchair next to the window waiting, and let the dark fill my room. About the same time, the wife switched on the living room lamps, and her husband pushed the on-button: the TV awoke with something between a yawn and a scream. Sometimes I even stayed up with them to watch the late late movie. It was summer, and when they left the windows open, I could hear the shouts, pleas, gunshots, and the strains of music that urged it all on. I could've just closed my eyes and listened, the music would've told me how to feel. But the words don't always match up with what's really going on, so I kept my eyes open just to make sure I wasn't missing anything.

He always came home at six-thirty, and she usually had dinner ready for him. They ate in the kitchen which I could only see at an angle. If I had really wanted to watch them eat, I would've had to stand on my toilet and open the small hinged window with the textured pane of glass and stick my head out a bit. When they were in their bedroom, their curtains were always closed. So I sat in my chair and waited for them to finish. I was happy to wait.

....

The apartment is small, sparse. Downstage a blush-red, soft sofa: a mouth whose lips are slightly parted, tongue curled inside, waiting for the right word to utter. A lacquered pine coffee table, slick, unscratched. Upstage a wall of empty shelves, but for the television at the center. One enormous, unblinking eye. The wood beneath it bends with its weight.

HE is tall, thirty-three with rolling shoulders that his wife can press her head into, feel surrounded by even if he does not embrace her.

SHE is blonde, zipper-teeth clenched tight. If HE holds her hands, her slender, restless fingers that make him nervous, she might not come undone. HE is afraid that those hands might do something. HE holds them often. When HE doesn't, her hands graze her thighs, her hips, her ribcage to just below her breasts with a tentative pulse, as if SHE is surprised to find her body where it is, nervously amused that it is actually there. When HE comes home in the evening, SHE is waiting for him. They are sitting on the sofa when SHE opens the curtains. SHE has her hands clenched between her thighs, fingers woven. HE sits forward, facing the television, not looking at her.

SHE: What do you want to do tonight?

HE: I don't know. What do you want to do?

SHE: I want to *not* do what we do every night.

HE: Okay, what then?

SHE: Something *different*.

HE: Like what?

SHE: You don't know? Guess. Guess what I want to do.

HE: I don't know, and I don't want to guess.

SHE: Then I don't know either. Forget it. We'll watch something.

SHE waits before getting up, deciding what SHE wants to watch. Nothing moves in the small apartment but her. Even the slight summer breeze is not strong enough to swing the open curtains. SHE watches him for a moment and sees a few brown hairs at the crown of his head lift and fall. Then SHE turns on the television, a roar like an engine turning over. SHE eases back into the sofa, thrusts her hands in his and feels the perspiration. SHE wonders if it's his wet or hers.

....

I thought I knew them pretty well because I knew what they liked to watch: movies mostly—old black and whites with heavy shadows and faces lit by swerving headlights or a single candle, Technicolor love stories that take place in little towns with changing seasons and strangers only passing through, and occasionally something new like an action flick. Romantics, but thrilled by an unexpected twist. Without the television on, they seemed agitated, as if they didn't know what to with each other. They also watched the news. Religiously, as if they expected to see their own faces flash on screen. She sat at the edge of the sofa, her head tilted up slightly as if to receive communion, and the light from the television shone, setting her hair on fire when there were wars and gun wounds and burning car wrecks.

I saw them when they first moved in, not so long ago, and the last thing they unpacked was the television. Everything they did seemed edged with passion—slow, comfortable deep strokes of a linen cloth over the empty shelves and tabletops to clean them. Sharp slices of a knife blade to open boxes. Deep, heavy, salt-moist breath while lifting and pushing the sofa against the window, the shelves against the other wall. Every inch of the apartment, an act of love. After everything was unpacked and in its place, I saw her restless, pacing, waiting to be injected with calm.

....

You thought you knew it pretty well by now, the pattern of the crime: a door busted in, furniture turned over, drawers emptied, blood, urine, and vomit streaked across the walls and floor as if her body had been turned inside out. It's what you hoped you'd find when the call came in about the rape. It's what you'd need to solve the case. Hard evidence. Without it, there would be only line-ups and a woman who silently looked through a one-way mirror anxious that he might see her, that, despite the glass plate, the steel cuffs, the uniformed men with batons and shiny badges, his hands might touch her again. You would only get a few reluctant words, whispers, as if the act of identifying him, of pointing at him and saying yes, that's him, would make her responsible for his existence, his act. You prayed there'd be more than that, as tragic as it'd be to see, though you'd seen it all before. You swallowed hard and closed your eyes before you pushed the door open with the palm of your hand. It swung gently on its hinges like a single page of a book turned by a breath of wind.

....

HE stands in the doorway, shaking out his umbrella. HE is wet, breathless from running in the rain. Water glistens like pearls on his long black raincoat. HE has caught her fingering the tulip's red petals, wide blossoms bent over the curled lip of the glass vase. When HE opened the door, SHE was on her knees, the thick of her belly and hips spread over her legs as she leaned across the coffee table to arrange the flowers. SHE turned her head toward him, as if to listen to the wet scrape of the folds of his umbrella.

HE would like to go to her, lift her, embrace her, kiss her— the wet chill of rain makes him ache for her warmth. But when SHE thrusts her hands in his direction, HE shivers. HE sees only her fingers moving—like a corpse, HE thinks, whose fingers twitch with the last electrical current traveling out of its body. Only impulse. HE runs his own hand from the steely pointed tip of his umbrella over the damp fabric and twists the folds and fastens them. Seeing that HE will not take her hands, SHE lifts herself slightly and places them beneath the round of her behind and holds her ankles tight. Then HE leans over and kisses her on the back of the neck.

SHE: I wish we weren't married.

HE: You wish we weren't married?

130

SHE: I mean, we are married. You know?

HE: Yes.

SHE: I just wonder if we weren't married whether mar riage would mean something to you.

HE: It does. It does mean something.

SHE: Does it mean that you, that you can forget I'm here, that I exist?

HE: No, it doesn't. I'm sorry. I forget myself. I don't forget you.

SHE: What can I do to remind you?

HE: You don't have to remind me.

HE goes to her, crouches behind her, a thigh on either side of her, wrapping his long arms around her, almost hugging himself. The thick peel of a fruit. The hard shell of an insect with a soft underbelly. SHE leans her head into his shoulders, but SHE doesn't know where to put her hands. They twitch, caught between her body and his. The curtains are open, and when they stand, SHE draws the cord and closes them.

....

Whenever she closed the curtains, I felt a little awkward like the shamed feeling of running to the post box and finding nothing in it. Or like when I see someone on the street is smiling at me, and I feel warm and smile back, only to discover that I haven't been seen at all.

The television wasn't even on that night. I saw him wrap himself around her from behind. Her body melt into his. I wanted to know if he'd let her turn around and kiss him. If he would take off her clothes slowly, his finger and thumb pushing each button through each hole, peeling back her shirt the way the loose skin of a mandarin falls away from its ripe flesh. If she pulled down his trouser zipper, or watched him do it himself. How she knew that he loved her.

This time when she closed the curtains, she seemed to say: I know you're watching. Like an invitation to wait for the next act. I could've left my chair and drawn my blinds, found something to do in my apartment. But I waited. I didn't want to miss anything. I watched the shadows dance to music I couldn't hear.

....

Every time's like the first time, and you had to admit there's a thrill, a rush like being the first five minutes in love: the nauseous sweet burn of a quick shot of scotch when it hesitates between your throat and your gut. When the door opened, you stood still, holding your breath, surveying the small apartment—a bed, a chest of drawers, a large orange armchair and a coffee table with a vase of flowers, all neatly pushed up against the walls, kitchenette directly to your right, bathroom door past the refrigerator, perpendicular to the window. Everything in its place. All the furniture, dusted for fingerprints, glowed white with powder, iridescent, a thousand hands had caressed every inch. Between the bed in the back corner and the armchair at the window, you saw a one-inch bloodstain on that wall five feet up and a splattered puddle below it. You exhaled. And in the next breath, the acid bite of urine prickled your nose. You knew it was too soon to tell whether it was his or hers. You walked through the bustle of uniformed men. You took pictures of the bloodstain, the urine, the drawers the others had opened: inside perfectly arranged clothes. Five matching pairs of underwear, all cotton, three white, baby blue, beige. Wool stockings, nylon hose, old leather gloves, and stacks of papers carefully tied with a blue silk ribbon. Love letters, you thought. Every time you took a picture, the blue flash emptied the room of life for a split second, a light so intense it froze all movement. You imagined a rose dipped in liquid nitrogen, its petals brittle, waiting to shatter. Someone told you that they tied her down to the gurney and took her to the ambulance outside. That she was calm and waiting to talk to you. You made your way to her, pushing your way through the crowd of neighbors in the hall and on the street who huddled in nightclothes. Red and blue light from the squad cars traveled across their faces like the rhythmic pumping of blood out of and into the heart. It was dark inside the ambulance, but you could see the thick blanket, strapped across in two places, her head turned to the side, and her hands—her finger spread wide as if to touch everything, nothing.

....

HE looks at his watch. It throbs on his wrist like an engorged heart clamped, ready for surgery. HE was late coming home. HE forgot the time, forgot his hunger. SHE has made him dinner. HE is very late, and will not tell her that HE is not hungry. HE knows that SHE has been cooking for hours. HE smells hot oil, pepper, her sweat. HE knows that off-stage SHE has put a cast-iron skillet on the stove and chopped vegetables. That SHE pulled a whole chicken out of the refrigerator, rinsed it, dug out the innards and sawed off the neck. Pulled each leg out and cut through the slick skin and fat. Then each wing, each thigh. SHE cracked the ribcage with a knife, then took the breasts in her hands and bent them in and out, as if teaching the dead bird how to fly again, until the breasts split. SHE dredged each piece in cornmeal, crumbs, flour, and black pepper, while the oil she poured in the skillet pooled above the blue hiss of flames. Dinner is ready, and HE wonders what she does with the innards. They never eat them. HE does not know what they taste like. HE says nothing.

SHE: You know I love you. You know that, don't you?

HE: Yes. I know you do.

They sit down for dinner. HE eats very little, picking at his food, tearing the fried skin off the chicken and stabbing the breast with his fork. SHE eats, not because SHE is hungry, but to show him that it is good, that HE should eat. If SHE eats, perhaps HE will eat. SHE stuffs hot pieces of meat into her mouth, tearing the flesh off the bone, then SHE licks each greasy finger with such rapture, HE thinks, SHE might eat herself.

HE gets up and goes to the living room. SHE clears the table and her hands are shaking. SHE is angry that HE did not eat what SHE spent all afternoon fixing. HE is in the living room now, but the television is not on. The silence shocks her, and with a swipe of her arm, SHE breaks a half-filled wine glass. As SHE collects the shards from the floor, a sliver of glass cuts her finger. SHE puts it in her mouth. The taste of her blood is so familiar to her. SHE wonders if HE knows what SHE tastes like. SHE enters the living room, and offers him her finger, for a Band-aid, a kiss. HE is looking out the window.

HE: There's a woman over there watching us. Did you know there was a woman across the street watching us?

SHE: Yes.

HE: How long have you known? How could you have let her watch us?

SHE: Close the curtains then if it makes you nervous.

HE: I will not close the curtains. That woman should not be watching us. I will not close the curtains. This is my home. I should be able to open and close the curtains when I want.

SHE: Leave the curtains open then and ignore her. Or we can go into the bedroom where she won't see us. Do you want to do that?

HE: No.

Her finger is still bleeding. HE watches drops of blood drip onto the coffee table. HE takes her hand by the wrist, pulls her to him on the sofa, inspects her finger then puts it in his mouth. Her blood tastes like his. HE wants to kiss her, but when HE looks out the window across the street, HE sees the woman's face peering from the edge of the window frame. That woman is watching him, studying his every gesture for its meaning. If I kiss her, HE thinks, there will be no doubt. HE kisses his wife —a long deep kiss that his mouth remembers suddenly, as if an idea long gone has finally found the right words.

....

He was sitting in the living room alone. I was waiting for him to turn on the television. But instead he stared out the window. It was already late, past dusk on a summer night, and though he seemed to be looking straight at me, I thought he was only able to see his reflection in the glass, a jaundiced yellow from the bright bulbs. His jaw was clenched, the muscles in his face taut, eyes open wide. I stared back because I felt sure he couldn't see me. I felt I might almost see my own face in his, the way we were staring, as in a mirror, looking past the whole face, losing oneself in the shape of an earlobe, in the quick contraction of a pupil, in the gold feathering of a green iris.

134

Then, with a blink, remembering the entire face.

Then the wife came in, and he pointed in my direction, jerking his head back and forth between us. She stood there with one finger outstretched, not accusingly, but like an angel or a saint that has touched a holy relic and offers up the power of it. She was calm, still, graceful in that moment when she lifted her head to look straight at me.

I was always careful to keep my lights off so that I could watch their television clearly. Part of me wanted to flick on the light-switch. Reveal myself and show them who I was. Another part of me, wanted to close my eyes in the dark and imagine her face without having to look in her eyes, without having to see her. But instead, I pushed my head up against my armchair, so that my face was partly hidden, and kept looking and they gave me a kiss.

....

After he left, after she locked the door, after she called the police, she waited, she said. She did not shower, did not touch herself. She promised. She told you this from the gurney where a wool blanket covered her almost naked body. She would not tell you exactly what happened, but you knew. You'd seen these cases often enough to know exactly. But you needed her testimony if the evidence made the case unclear. There were questions you had to ask: how well did she know him? how often had he been to her apartment? when and where had they first met? had they had sex before? how often? You sounded like a jealous lover. She had every right not to answer.

....

HE: What do you want to do tonight?
SHE: I don't know.
HE: Let's not watch television.
SHE: What then?
HE: I want you to seduce me.
SHE: What do you want me to do?
HE: I want you to let me watch you undress.

SHE: I want you to hold my hands behind my back.

HE: I want you to open your eyes and look at me while we fuck.

SHE: I want you to eat me and then kiss me so I'll know what I taste like.

HE: I want to leave the curtains open.

SHE stands on the coffee table before him, her fingers work the pearl buttons on her blouse, releasing each from the stitching until her bare midriff and white bra are exposed between the open drapes of silk. SHE reaches to her waist to unzip her skirt, but it catches. SHE pulls down hard on the zipper. It will not come undone. SHE fights it, tugging hard, almost in tears for the shame of being caught. HE takes her hips in his arms and pulls her toward him, so that SHE's standing on her knees straddling him on the sofa, and HE lifts her skirt up on to her hips. Her face, almost pressed against the window, is contorted with the anguished rapture of letting him in to a place SHE has never been. SHE reaches with one outstretched hand to close the curtains, and HE grabs her hand and twists it behind her back. The curtains stay open.

....

They knew I was watching. They left the curtains open. They let me in, embraced me, showed me, but there was only silence. I touched myself, found places on my body that I had forgotten the names for, as if my skin spoke another language. My fingers were wet, the lips of my cunt contracting, but no sound came out. I was afraid I would scream. Isn't that what love is, anyway—being touched into existence, that no part of you is real until it is touched? I say I love you, and you are touched everywhere.

....

You walked beside her as she was wheeled from the ambulance down the hospital corridor and into the examination room. You held her up just above her elbow as she stood, then a nurse cut off her panties with a pair of scissors. Another nurse took her arm. You loaded the film into the Polaroid, pulled the white strip out, and aimed. The nurses turned her around slowly, her feet sticking to the cold linoleum floor. In the viewfinder you found the gash on the crown of her head, then the bruises on the nape of her neck, below her underarms, around her wrists. The camera spat the pictures onto the floor. Her thighs filled the square window that you squinted through: cuts and scrapes, red and black. The nurses sat her down at the edge of the table and pulled her knees apart. You crouched between her legs. You saw that she was bleeding. You marked the pictures with a black pen: upper ribcage, left wrist, right thigh.

The doctor arrived, and the nurses put her feet up in the stirrups. A cold speculum was inserted into her distended vagina, a thick cotton swab followed, and then the speculum was removed. The doctor, with rubber gloves coated in K-Y jelly warmed on the electric pad, put his hand inside her up to the wrist. She looked at you. You were still watching.

....

They are pacing in front of the window, strutting, panting, knowing they are being watched. SHE pulls the cord down and the curtains swing closed, like a hasty jerk of the rope when someone backstage thinks something's gone very, very wrong. But HE opens them again, cannot decide whether to turn to her in his shouting, or face front to the audience. HE projects well, carefully. SHE is all sighs, and high-pitched pleas.

SHE: Enough. It's enough now.
HE: It didn't seem to make any difference to you before.
SHE: It does now. Please close the curtains.
HE: No. I told you that woman will not dictate whether or not my curtains are open. If she wants to watch us, let her watch. I have nothing to hide. As a matter of fact, I'm happy to have her watch.
SHE: That's what it is, isn't it—that she's watching.
HE: And what is she to you?
SHE: I want to know if you love me.

His mouth stretches open, but no words come out. HE's

forgotten his lines, HE looks as if his tongue is paralyzed or cut from his mouth. HE looks at ME across the street. Stares straight at ME because HE knows I'm watching. I stare back because I've memorized this scene. If I were on-stage, I would know exactly what to do, what to say. I would take her in my arms and kiss her, and tell her I loved her. Put her hands around my neck, where her fingers could graze hungrily in my hair, travel down my spine, so SHE could know that there's another standing before her, touching her body, too, and that we exist. I open my window and reach out my arms and throw my voice out like roses, like lilies tossed at a performer's feet.

I: Tell her you love her.

HE looks at me as if HE has not understood, as if he did not quite hear what HE wanted to hear. I scream.

I: Tell her you love her.

HE says nothing. HE looks at his wife who stands before ME like my reflection quivering in cold clear water. I want to dive in and not open my eyes, just feel the water parting, swallowing me. I'd breathe it in, take it in my lungs till my blood was full of it, my heart pumping it, and my mouth would be full and I would not be able to speak.

....

You wanted to know what happened. Exactly what happened. You needed to know so that you could put the pieces together, get the story straight, make the arrest, and lock him up. I've been trying to tell you. I've tried the best I could because as it all happened it became memory, memory imagined in each second after the second it happened, and I tried to lock the memory into words, but I could only see it in my mind like a home movie spliced, cut. Afterward, when he was gone, it was so quiet and I closed my eyes, watching it happen again and again, but at a distance, watching it outside myself, watching someone else hear the knock, expecting him, having waited for him. She had arranged flowers on the table, cleaned house, made him dinner, lit candles. Her heart throbbed in her throat, excited as she heard the bolt slide out with a clack, the doorknob click. Light from the hallway spilled in, she could not see his face, until he closed the door and turned on the lights. She let him in. Everything went still in that moment, there was only the quake and hum of light. A light so bright, as if she were suddenly on-stage, the curtains and expectations up, a thousand faces shrouded in darkness watching, waiting for her to recite every line she had rehearsed. She forgot all the words. When she let him in. It happened like this:

He stood behind her and wrapped one arm around her waist. It pinched back her arms tightly. With his other hand, he covered her mouth, and she stiffened as he pulled her head hard against his shoulder, twisting her head away from her body. She leaned in to him, as he led her across the room, holding the curve of her back into his hard-breathing belly. Her feet stumbled, ankles twisting, until he spun her around and threw her against the wall. Her head fell back, knocked the wall twice. She sunk to the floor, her mouth open, tongue too thick to speak.

The steel swish of a zipper grated on her teeth as she clenched her jaw, thinking that she would, like a dog, swallow her tongue. Her eyes were open as she saw the loose cut of his pants tighten as he bent toward her, the palm of his hand pushing her into the wall. She did not know what to do with her own hands, they felt heavy but agitated like a fever pulsed through them, made them thick, enormous, immobile. He said to her, Tell me you love me. Say you love me, bitch. Bile rose up her gut, her muscles contracted. Say YOU LOVE ME, he said as he gripped her around the neck just below the jaw. I love you, she whispered, as if she had been wanting to say it all along.

....

SHE: Enough. It's enough now.
HE: It didn't seem to make any difference to you before.
SHE: It does now. Please close the curtains.
HE: No. I told you that woman will not dictate whether or not my curtains are open. If she wants to watch us, let her watch. I have nothing to hide. As a matter of fact, I'm happy to have her watch.
SHE: What is it that you want her to see?

HE: That I love you. It's you I love. You know that, don't you?
SHE: I know now. I love you, too.

....

Even now he is still touching me. He was still touching me when he left. When I lay in bed alone, I couldn't even hold myself. I felt his hands all over me. I couldn't touch myself. Was afraid that if I didn't, I wouldn't be sure that my body was still there. But I couldn't. I lay flat—stretched out so that no skin touched skin, and I curled up into a ball inside that skin, sinking deep into my body, holding my skin out away from me with my fingers, elbows, and toes, so if he was still touching me, I'd be faraway enough from my skin not to feel it.

....

Since that night I've been down on my knees scrubbing the wood floor with hard, circular swipes of rags of ripped shirts and old underwear, scratching out the lint, crumbs, nail clippings between the floorboards, fingers and corn husk broom probing each crack. Emptying the dresser of all my clothes, piling it high, washing, drying, ironing towels, shirts, sheets, panties. I've cleaned the toilet bowl, the sink, the drain, picking out each stray hair. I know every inch of this place, I know it blind. I keep my lights off. I am exhausted every night when I turn my television on to listen to the words. I always turn down the contrast so that the small screen turns from bright to gray to black. Dust prickles with the last bit of light from the screen. Sometimes I think I hear voices from behind me, from the window, and I am careful not to turn around, but when I do, I see a slightly familiar face, dim and gray, reflected in the glass, all lights out across the street.

Laura Mullen

His Father

Laura Mullen is the author of *The Surface*, which was chosen for the National Poetry Series by C.K. Williams and published by the University of Illinois in 1991. Her work has appeared in *Agni, Antaeus, Bomb, The Colorado Review, The New Yorker, notus, Pataphysics, Volt*, and other magazines. She was awarded *Ironwood's* Stanford Prize in 1983, and has been the recipient of Fellowships from the National Endowment for the Arts and the MacDowell Colony. She is currently on the graduate faculty at Colorado State University.

His Father

Far away from here his father is bronzing the dogs, I'm sure of it, I'm suddenly sure: he's bronzing the hunting dogs and the house dogs and his wife's horses, in pieces, and as for his wife—his mother—I just have to hope he can't catch her. Along with the other children. He doesn't want anything to happen. Especially this. Us. Well, we knew that all along.

On the road up to the house our mouths went dry from nervous tension. "My father...," he said. He didn't have to finish. He wouldn't like it. We knew all along.

Or his father is out there on the lawn calling down the forces we always suspected he was at least secretly connected with, if not in charge of. Men in dark glasses, with tight mouths and hands riding light and easy on their weapons, step out of the helicopter onto the lawn. And look all around. Silent.

It's fall, it's already cold there.

He said: "He's crazy, you know that."
I said: "I don't care, I just want to go home."

Far away his father is taking the guns down, out from behind the locked door, the false wall. The expensive, irreplaceable guns. Handmade in England, most of them. For him. For the journeys to foreign countries the trophies are brought back from. He's taking them down, oiling them, loading them, he calls out to one of the dogs, an encouraging call, "C'mon!"

He could see how he was like his father, and must have thought I would also, sooner or later. His father's fear, couldn't we stop talking about it? His fear, then. Or my fear. The unfinished sentence. We kept coming back to it. Everything told to be good, to be still. Tolling like bells when we banged on the metal skin, shining and hollow. I said, "I just want something stable for once, something I can count on."

In his dream he's the dog. His father and older brothers aim above him. The birds fall. "Isn't it," I had to ask, "too simple?"

The woods behind the house reddening even now.

The helicopter makes that *whup,whup,whupping* sound. His father wants us to be quiet, to be very quiet. We could cry, but we're too frightened. And we're not supposed to feel.

He said: "You don't understand, you h*ave* to lie to him."
I said: "I don't believe that."

The electronic collars. The lovely property fenced invisibly with high-pitched noises and jolting shocks. His father holding onto the controls. And when he says "Halt...."

The birds fall. The woods redden. How could I be homesick? We knew all along. How could I go looking for love there? His father, of course, an avid photographer. Behind him the dark blue ocean, the wooden deck of the boat. "Don't you miss it?" I ask. He hates to cry. But he says, "I was always the one left out." Held up in the air, in picture after picture, the glittering catch, stilled, thrashes and chokes.

He thought I thought he was like his father, probably, and couldn't bear....

He thought there was something I was attracted to, yes, in this man who wanted everything finished, everything under control. The smell of damp earth and rotting leaves and his father shaking his head, "Not good, not good." Or "An infatuation, merely." How could I prove I wasn't in love? What could I use to show....

Far away from here his father turns on the TV. A little peace, that's all....

He can hear the thud of the suddenly heavy bodies falling from out of the air above his head and into the undergrowth. There's the scent of blood. Was he trained for this? Was he trained well enough?

Far away his father is waiting by the phone, a newspaper rolled in his hand, "What's wrong?" he says, "What's wrong now?" "How are your teeth?" He demands, "Have you done what I asked you to do?"

It's football season. It's hunting season. The beautiful property dangerous. The air cracking open. Off the granite outcrop the sound of the shots reverberates. The shivering leaves, the deep chill. "Don't you miss it, just a little?"

The dogs are bronzed, the horses too, it was hard work, but yes. I know. He pats his wife on his way back to the couch, *clank*. The children ring true. I suddenly know. Far away from here his father sits down in front of the TV, feet up, newspaper open, reading glasses resting on the end of his nose, eyes shut. On the gleaming surfaces reflecting him back his sigh—of satisfaction—is a dull brief bloom. The helicopter floats back into the clear blue above the gold and rust and bronze of the the dying leaves, the stubble in the wide meadows. It must be satisfaction. From here everything—like the ocean seen from a long way up—glistening and still.

Nicolette De Csipkay

The Cat Lady

Nicolette De Csipkay received an MA in Creative Writing from the University of Colorado in 1986. Currently ABD for a Ph.D. in English from SUNY Buffalo, she is sharing a teaching position with her husband at Lakeland College in Sheboygan, Wisconsin. Most recently, her fiction has been published in *Gulf Coast*, *Short Story*, and *Rohwedder*.

The Cat Lady

Bored with teachers who flittered false eyelashes, sick of girls who answered their questions, and tired of girls who liked boys and boys who liked girls, Janet was passing by rows of glossy-leaved orange trees on her way home from a tenth-grade school day when she saw a small man with dark hair, a moustache and very muscular arms digging a pit in the backyard of the house with the rooster weathervane. He was listening to a soft pop radio station, but as Janet walked by he looked up and gestured to her.

"Need some extra cash?" he asked.

"No," Janet mumbled uncertainly. "I have to go do my homework." She added this in a garbled manner, so that the man did not understand her and interpreted her answer to be affirmative. Janet was a shy girl, but she had also learned that mumbling allowed her a certain freedom—the freedom to do what she wanted regardless of what she said. Janet changed words at will, misunderstanding or being misunderstood as it suited her.

"I have a sister," the man went on, "a sister who likes girls like you. Do you know any boys? She also likes boys."

Janet shook her head, but the man was already opening the gate into the backyard. From next to the shovel blared a static-ridden Tom Jones song, and the man stooped to turn down the volume. "Come in," he said heartily. "Kids like you can always use a little extra cash. And it won't be much work, no," he shook his head, laughing, "not work like I have here." He jerked his head in the direction of the pit. Janet could not help her curiosity, so she followed the man into the house.

The house smelled sweet, like overripe bananas or maybe apples, but slightly nauseating to Janet because just beneath the smell there were lots of kittens milling about and two overflowing litterboxes. "My sister's in the back room," the man said, jerking his head at the wall, "but you can have something to eat first. You must be hungry after school." He took Janet's school books from her and put them on the kitchen table. "Do you like cheddar?" Janet nodded; she liked cheese. "Good," said the man, opening the refrigerator, "we've had this since last Christmas, and my sister won't eat it because she's allergic to lactic acid, and I like my hamburgers plain." The man took out a big oblong cardboard box and opened it up. "This is government cheese," the man said. "We have food stamps, too." Inside the box the cheese was covered with green mold. Matter-of-factly he took the cheese in his hand, scraped it with a knife, and then carved off a large piece for Janet. But Janet only pretended to eat it because she didn't like blue unless it was supposed to be there and once it was there you couldn't take it away. "Just a minute," said the man, "I'll go talk to my sister." When he left Janet threw the piece of cheese into an earthenware jar on top of the television in the living room.

She stroked one of the kittens. It had grey and white patches and blue eyes; it was very young and tried to suck at her fingers.

"Okie-dokie," she heard the man say, and then he came into the living room. "Go down the hall, last door to the right. My sister will tell you want she wants."

Janet put down the kitten carefully and it ran under the sofa.

The man's sister was a big fat lady lying in bed. She was naked and she had another kitten draped across her breast, pure black and purring like a pinwheel. Janet stopped at the doorway and stared at her until the lady looked up. "My you're a quiet one," she said. "Come on in and sit down, sweetie," she said, patting the bed by her side. "Do you like kittens," she said, "do you want to pet my kitty?" Janet nodded because she didn't know what to say. She petted the lady's kitten until it started to meow and began pulling itself towards her, its claws digging for a hold in the woman's soft flesh. "Naughty, naughty," the woman said, gently detaching his claws and putting him next to her on the bed, "you know better than to do that to Mama." The lady's sheets were mostly blue, with little white flowers on them.

The lady took Janet's hand and held it. "Do you have a boyfriend, sweetie?" she said. "M-mm," Janet answered. The lady put her hand on her stomach. "I have a fat tummy, don't I?" She wore a blue satin ribbon around her neck. "Do you know why? Feel my stomach," the lady said. "There—can you feel it kicking? Feel it again. Can you feel it in there?" she asked insistently. Janet looked steadily at the lady's forehead; she felt nothing, except that the lady's skin was soft, covered with a powdery, silky down. The lady prompted her hand further along. "Can you feel it here?" Janet shook her head. "Here?" "No, here," she corrected herself, "just keep your hand here and I know you'll feel it."

The lady pressed Janet's hand close to her body and Janet didn't dare move it. She saw the lady's eyelashes flutter almost shut and her mouth open slightly, her lips dark red and glistening. In the next room there were a few coughs, a toilet flush, a faucet's squeak on and off. Janet felt something move beneath her hand. The lady made a choking noise. "Did you feel it?" she gasped, "did you feel it?" Janet nodded. "Another little one just dying to get out!" the lady said with delight. "And aren't you just a good kid? I just bet a good kid like you would go out there and bring me one of my babies back. You know the cutie with the blue eyes? It's about his dinner time. Then you can go home if you want, sweetie, just tell my brother and he'll give you the cash."

Janet searched high and low, but she couldn't find the kitten and finally had to ask the man. "Give her this," he directed, and she took the small tiger-striped one he handed her into the lady. "Thanks, sweetie," she said, putting the kitten's mouth to her nipple, "you be sure to come back and visit us again."

Janet left the room and asked the man for money. He reached in the earthenware jar where she had thrown the cheese. "You don't like our cheese? It's not good enough for you?" he growled, spitting on the ground and throwing her an angry glance. He pulled out a handful of quarters from the jar and held them out to her. "Now get out of here. Just get out," he repeated more quietly, looking away. Janet took the money and picked up her books.

On her way to the gate she saw a huddle of kittens at the bottom of the pit the man had been digging, the grey and white kitten curled up into a little ball on top, fast asleep. The rooster on the roof spun with a sudden whir, and Janet lifted the ponytail off of her neck. She clicked her tongue and called out "kitty," but it didn't move.

"It's no use, kid," the man said, coming from behind her and picking up the spade. "She just has too damn many of them. I just can't afford it anymore."

When Janet got home her mother was anxious. "You're late. Your father will be home any minute and you know how angry he'd be if you hadn't been here."

"Well, I am here. I just went to Howard Johnson's with Evie for awhile, that's all," Janet mumbled.

"What's that? Well, you better be careful young lady, I'm warning you," her mother put her hands on her hips. "By the way, the Lenders called wondering if you could babysit to-night."

"Okay," Janet said, going into her room and shutting the door. She emptied the change out of her purse and clunked it into the fat belly of her piggy bank.

Between five and six on weekday evenings, if the sun had not set, you could look down from Janet's window on a lush green expanse of orange groves and on the sparkling, double strand of cars traveling perpetually elsewhere. Beyond that you could see the mountains rising sharply into the sky, and somewhere above that all the extra money Janet would earn and the day she would have a car like everyone else.

But a beautiful blue car with an eight-track tape-deck and windows you could open and shut by button.

Jonis Agee

Mustard

Jonis Agee grew up in the Midwest and has spent most of her life coming to understand that there is something surreal there. She has published three collections of fiction, *Bend This Heart*, *Pretend We've Never Met*, and *.38 Special and A Broken Heart*; three novels, *Salvation's Sister*, *Strange Angels*, and *Sweet Eyes*; and a volume of poetry, *Houses.* She teaches creative writing at the University of Michigan.

Mustard

It wasn't until I started answering the phone, hello, where are you on the food chain, that I figured I'd better get out of Dodge. I kept hoping it'd be his girlfriend, and she'd answer truthfully, higher than you, honey. No such luck. It was always some guy realizing his mistake immediately and pretending that the Amos he was looking for, wasn't the one I'd lost. Fat chance, I muttered each time and went back to my solitaire game. It haunted me a little bit, this card business, like it was really some kind of family business, like the trouble I was in now. My grandfather shared some of these same troubles, love, and by the time he died, the figures on his deck of cards were almost worn clean away. Maybe he just knew them so well after a while, he didn't even have to look at the numbers.

The bargain I made was that I'd get over Raul by the time I hit Albert Lea. That was 90 miles away and since we'd only been sleeping together for four months, it seemed far enough. But it took me all the way to Des Moines, cursing through sleet and rain, trying to avoid the Iowa state troopers who have a lookout for people such as me, and all of Dwight Yoakam's sad ass songs bleating away like they were trapped in the back of the pickup with the tv, loveseat and trunk that had belonged to my grandfather, the one I mentioned before. I couldn't leave anything called a loveseat behind, even though it matched the sofa in our little house like a man and wife pair before the picture window that looked out over the tucked under drive-way and garage. Amos would just have to make do, hell, he probably liked it side by side with his girlfriend, staring at the Weber grill like it was the president making a speech.

Raul was a later addition to my life, and always had that hasty, jerryrigged feeling like he'd been plastered on to the side of the house on weekends by relatives and you could still see where the lousy carpentry took place, where the lines didn't quite square and meet. He was the best I could do under emergency conditions. And we're not a family prone to complaining. I just wasn't prepared to have my heart broken twice, like two car wrecks in one day, the odds are just plain against that kind of thing happening, aren't they.

The cows were nosing the new green fields, grateful as all get out, but that didn't cheer me any. The baby horses were lying on their sides too tired to think about anything when the sun shone, which it did in between storms. I've always liked those spring storms about the best, the way they come floating up the horizon like big boats trying to get across the sky. They're not as heavy and vicious as summer storms and usually I just enjoy the heck out of them. Raul was on my mind though, and in the back of my throat, the way he'd shoved it in there that time, deeper and deeper against my gagging. I was trying to find how people could love each other these days, I figured after all those years being married to Amos, I'd lost track of things. And strangely, it did work, I felt like some porn star making men come in their pants in those worn out slick chairs in the smelly place up on Lake Street in Minneapolis Amos took me a couple of times when we were trying to wring some more out of that tired t-shirt we called our marriage. It was Raul who knew how to make the movie come on in my head though, and I was sure going to miss it, that's what I was thinking from Albert Lea to Des Moines as I was saying goodbye to all that hot sex business.

The road from Des Moines to Kansas City was pretty empty except for a few single men in cars older than mine that said they too had their share of such troubles. Thinking Amos away was harder, and I guess I knew it might take all of Missouri and part of Arkansas or Louisiana just to sweat him out. The land moving south gets hilly and woody, like it's letting you know things are changing, that's what I like about it, even in May when the trees have that bright green outlook that's so damn perky you want to slap its face and send it to bed. I counted five shades of green and some pretty yellowy stuff that had to be a honey locust, but I put it in a class of its own, along with weepy willows. Osceola, Iowa was the same as last time when I drove through with Amos to check on grandfather's farm, the one he'd always owned and never worked. Maybe that's where things went wrong, him going out there to see how the farmer was doing, staying too long when the wife was there alone and grandma and I were tucked away safely at the drugstore in town having our malteds and waiting. Maybe he should've worked the farm, I mean, at least helped out by leaving the wife alone. Can't a person go to work anymore, send another person to work, and expect they'll come home about the same as when they left, that home will be about the same too as when they left? What's it mean if safety like that disappears from the world.

Pulling back on I-35 I wonder just for a moment, I don't let myself dwell on this because I've made a promise to only think certain things once through before I get over them, but I do let myself wonder what Amos's face is going to look like when he sees I'm gone in a few hours when he gets home from work. When he sees that I beat him to it, I mean. And that I took the tv and the loveseat and my grandfather's trunk and the two bank accounts except for two hundred dollars to pay the Sears bill I know is coming. I left that in a note too. Pay the Sears bill or they'll take back the sofa. We'd waited years for that sofa and loveseat, and maybe if we'd bought two sofas like the floor manager said, we'd still be together, because it was just like she'd warned us, two people always end up fighting about who gets the sofa, loveseats are just too short to accommodate comfortably.

I have to be honest about this. A person can probably guess it wasn't a sofa that drove Amos into the arms of the cpa at work, or Raul, for that matter, into the hands of his hairdresser. Of course, the sofa had nothing to do with Raul, with him it was always a shop and go kind of deal. I doubt that furniture ever has anything to do with these things, not the bed we tossed and turned away from each other in, not the tvs we kept buying in larger and larger sizes as if we could make that screen cough up something we needed after a while. What I started noticing were the pores on the backs of the models' hands on the shopping channels, and the stray hairs in the noses of the announcers on the all day news programs. You shouldn't get that close to another person, I decided, that's why I took the old 19 inch from the spare bedroom.

I could tell at this point I was in danger of feeling too sorry for myself, and concentrated on the two or three hawks, red tails I believe, who drifted overhead. It was impossible to tell whether they were hunting or just enjoying the columns of air they found drafting up from the ground below them. I had to wonder if my travel was contributing just a little bit, too, or if I was just another object moving on a grid below them, being sorted by size and taste. I'd seen the way a hawk dropped its head and stared straight down as it swooped, the curve of beak like another claw closed in concentration. The idea that they might be mating made me turn back to the empty road where the shattered shells and red spills of turtles began to appear. On either side the road dropped into marsh busy with red winged blackbirds hollering from tops of last years' cattails blown ragged and yellow. It was easy to see why the turtles might want to get away, but I suspected they were just trying to get across to their own egg laying which involved the double fatalism of love and traffic.

Amos had been seeing his cpa for more than budgetary concerns longer than I wanted to think about. The first time it came up, he said it was only a few weeks, but the truth aged rapidly, and the next time I asked, he got amnesia and confessed to months and months. It was staggering, like installments on a mortal disease. I felt like things were never going to be true again, like the calendar had taken on leggy growth the way johnny jump ups do when they get loose in your yard. Did she do the taxes at least, that was all I could say when the fourteen months rolled out of his mouth, like there had to be something beneficial out of all this. At the grocery store they let you buy cheap knife sets and bath towels at a discount while they rip you off at the register.

Though I was over Raul officially, I couldn't help comparing the two. Both of them had found women useful in the world, I could say that. All I did was part-time school teaching to seventh and eighth graders who threw their books out the windows when I turned my back. I knew they were going to do it, that's why I couldn't stop myself. It was like we both had to play along. They needed to show what they did to substitutes and I needed to show I wasn't quite good enough to be their real teacher. I suppose someone with that kind of attitude can't compete with people with real jobs. Like my grandfather, whose ashes are in that trunk in the back of the truck wedged between the tv and the loveseat in the spring floral pattern we took because it was a floor model on sale and all we could afford though I've noticed they always do spring florals in pinks and yellows and greens that are just a little too bright so they make the biggest statement in the house about what's what, and maybe it's all advertising for Sears so people will say where'd you get that sofa and you say, oh, Sears.

My grandfather got the farm in Iowa during the depression when the county ran out of money to pay him for being principal one year to its poor rundown schools hardly anyone could afford to send their kids to for want of shoes and coats and such to begin with. The land is a lot poorer down near the Missouri border, and that particular farm had been abandoned for a year when the county gave it over. He put a family in there, and immediately began seeing the wife, and later the daughter until the county suggested he keep the farm but take himself over the border to Nebraska to another job. He often left a place richer than when he came, a small trail of troubled hearts like dropped or abandoned flowers in his wake. At least that's the way I came to believe in him. Now I don't know of course.

Stopping for gas just over the border in some little Missouri town I forgot to read the sign for, I checked the stuff in back to make sure it hadn't shifted around too much. Everything looked fine, my clothes in the green garbage bags holding the tv in their arms with the blank screen staring grayly out at the world like a baby over its mother's shoulder. My grandfather was packed with pillows and comforters to keep him from sloshing over. I'd always meant to do something about him, and I suppose if Amos wanted to hold one thing over my head, it would be the old man coming to live with us like that. I was the only one in the family who wasn't pissed at him though, so I had to do it. I just couldn't decide what to do after that. I mean, nobody would have him in the family plots and he didn't seem the type to just be dumped out in the wind. He like being indoors, in dark rooms with women, what should I do, I used to shout at Amos, take him to a motel?

Oh, that wasn't the problem, not really. And that's one thing Janine and I agreed on in those little therapy sessions where she'd wait for me to break down crying and I'd feel responsible every time I made her unhappy because I didn't. We're not the type to spread our troubles around, I told her so she wouldn't feel like a failure. The day Amos and Raul told me enough was enough, I went to my appointment like I always did, five minutes early so she'd see I was a good client. Janine talked about herself for a few minutes, like she always did, which I encouraged her to do so she'd feel comfortable, and then told me she thought we'd do better as friends or something. She'd thought a lot about it, see, and I could see someone else if I wanted, or we could just hang out and be buddies now.

Janine wasn't a regular therapist, I have to admit that. I don't think she had anything more than the degree from the Psychic Institute of The West, which hung in a gold leaf frame above the futon where she kept trying to get me to meditate. I liked her because she had a signed picture of Frank Zappa and the Mothers of Invention hanging beside it and she'd always encourage me to follow my heart and have as much sex as I wanted and needed with Raul after I couldn't get Amos to pay me any mind.

When I told her about both men leaving me, she raised her eyebrows and tossed her fine blonde hair over her shoulder, and told me not to worry, it was just nature's way. We lit a candle then and practiced focussing, drank some bottled water, went to the bathroom down the hall to pee and tell dirty jokes from adjoining stalls where I had the urge to scrape something in the thick old green paint on the door, maybe Raul's telephone number, and then we hugged and I left.

Leaving the gas station, the truck coughed and chugged a little starting out in the new thicker, southern air that felt as if it was never going to be dry again, not ever. I wondered what Janine was going to do when I didn't call like I promised, when

I didn't go to her house for dinner next week, when I didn't show up at the Upper Midwest Psychic Fair to hold down the booth we rented as a group of her clients to show what's possible in the field of psychotherapy and psychic healing, when no matter how hard she tried to find my vibrations on the plains of her body, she wouldn't be able to. I wondered what Amos would do when she called to find out what happened. Or Raul, because I gave her those numbers, those clues to my life. If she was any kind of expert, she should come up with something, don't you think?

It sounds like I wanted to be found, doesn't it. Found and taken back to face the music. But I don't think that's true. I have to believe that when a person finds the test of time and safety just a bomb rigged to go off in her face, well, she has a right, even an obligation, say, to toss the books out the window and climb out after them. I'd sat around that house just long enough to figure out the mysteries of household appliances, furniture and love. I was eating a mustard sandwich, that was all, and it tasted just like you'd expect, mustard, yellow and bitter. And the further south I went, crossing border after border all the way to Mississippi, the more I felt like what I was really eating was a little piece of my heart, each step of the way. By the time I saw the Gulf, I vowed I'd forget all about those two men and just heave that urn into those dark choppy waters, and watch grandfather somehow find buoyancy and float away.

Lara Anderson Love

Skittles

Lara Anderson Love received her MFA in 1992 from the writing program at UC Irvine. Currently she is a radio talk show host for a weekly program called Mother Talk. She lives in Aptos, California, with her husband and three children.

Skittles

She suggested they play a game. It was the only fair way to decide. "But this is serious," Kurt begged. "This is our future. You and me not a game." He followed her down the hall towards the game room. "Look," he yelled after her, "It's fine to play Scrabble to decide where to go to dinner; if we can spell it we'll go there harmless and fun, right?" She turned the corner and passed through the library. "It's even fine that I had to play Probe with your parents before I could go out with you. But it is not, and I repeat, not, fine to play a game about this!" She walked into the game room. "Marriage is not a game!" he yelled, but she had already closed the door.

She was reaching for it when he walked in; the old one, not the newer version. The originals were all on the walls, on individual wood shelves with specially designed supports holding them up so the whole front of the box could be seen. They were all there, the family originals; Scrabble, Monopoly, Probe, Sorry, Clue, and Life. When Zella's parents were married, this was all they had, these six board games and a deck of cards. When Zella was six her mother killed herself, leaving only the word 'goodbye' written on the Scrabble board. These games were all Zella had growing up with her father; her only entertainment, her only taste of the outside world. They had been poor until Zella's father had invented his own game, Skittles. This stood on a separate marble table in a far corner of the room, and above it on the wall was a framed picture of Mr. Binette and the staff at Proctor & Gamble, holding a large cake with "Over One Million Served!" written in pink frosting.

"Why don't we play Skittles," Kurt said. "If I win we get

married." Kurt was the United States Skittles Champion three years in a row. He had met Zella at a Skittles Open Tournament in Kansas City. She was the referee, and he was the wildcard contender. He won twenty-five straight games in a row, and she defended him when a splinter group of The National Skittles Rules Committee accused him of cheating. They had been together ever since.

"This isn't a matter for Skittles," said Zella. "That's too random; things knocking into each other, reversing, and knocking into something else. This isn't a question of luck."

"I don't think your father would appreciate that definition."

"I'm going to play Life."

"Zella, we're talking about real life."

She shook her head and took the game off the shelf. "My parents played this to decide whether or not to have children. They had one child in the game, a pink girl." She walked over to the smallest marble table. "You can watch or not, it doesn't matter."

Kurt watched her set up her car, placing one pink peg in the driver's seat. He walked toward the door and turned back towards her. "Don't you think Old Maid would be a more appropriate game?" he asked, but Zella didn't answer. She had just become a Doctor—a guaranteed twenty thousand on every Pay Day.

He came back fifteen minutes later and she was in tears. "I lost everything. I was sued for malpractice, and then I gambled my inheritance on the stock market to pay for the gold mine, and I lost it. Everything. Gone." She looked up at him and started crying even harder. "And the fire," she put her and on her forehead, "I forgot to buy fire insurance."

Kurt looked down on her car, it was in the space marked Poor Farm. "It's alright," he said. Zella stood up and he encircled his arms around her like a straightjacket. "Everything is going to be okay." She cried into the space under his chin while Kurt consoled her. And over the top of her head he smiled, because sitting in the passenger's side of her little plastic car, was a tiny blue peg along for the ride.

Her father insisted on arranging things, and it wasn't until a week before the wedding that Kurt saw the special edition Skittles games that would adorn each table at the reception. Over the length of the game's normally plain but polished, miniature, wooden bowling pins, were tiny paintings of he and Zella in wedding dress. Their necks were the narrow tucks in the pins, and their faces swelled out from them at the top. Kurt picked up one of the pins with his face on it, and saw that except for the overly startled expression, it was almost identical.

"Do you want to play?" Zella's voice came over the intercom and settled in the game room.

Kurt looked at a large mirror on the wall in front of him. "How long have you been there?"

"Since before you came in."

"Doing what?"

"Watching. I was just watching."

Kurt held his miniature pin up to the mirror. "Did you see these?"

"Great, aren't they? Dad's giving one to everyone to take home from the wedding."

"I think it's sick. Whole families, for hours of fun and entertainment, will be knocking us down for the next twenty years." Kurt turned away from Zella and set his pin back on the game.

Skittles was a deceptively simple game and cheap to make. That was what had appealed most to the toy company. The game board was like a long, shallow box without its top. There were three sections divided by two horizontal wooden slats. In the first and third sections were two short vertical slats, with openings carved in so a top could spin through. These slats separated the pins in these sections, while the largest, middle section was completely open. The only way to get the top to spin from one section to the other was through one carved out slot in the first divider, and through two in the second.

Kurt aligned the six grooms across from six brides; one each in the first section, four in the second, and one in the third. "What's this?" He picked up the seventh pin. It was a painted Minister, and he placed it between the last two pins. This was the hardest pin to knock down and worth the most points because in order to knock it down you had to go through a special side opening in the third section.

"Are you going to play?"

Kurt nodded and picked up the top. It had a large diamond ring painted on. He picked the heaviest string and wound it carefully around the narrow base of the spinner and then back on itself a half turn.

"Which string are you using?

Kurt put the top just inside the game and pulled the loose end of the string out through a special hole in the front of the first section. He gave a little slack to the string and the top tilted forward toward the narrow opening in the wood, and then he quickly jerked back, solid and straight from his elbow. The string unwound in a flash and propelled the top straight through the first slot, bypassing the first bride and groom.

"Bravo."

The top spun straight down the middle section of the game, through the channel between the figures. It spun in place for a second then flew to the right, into the third section. Without knocking down the groom pin, it skimmed into the middle and sent the Minister flying through the left opening and right into the bride. Both pins flew up into the air and settled at the back of the game. Two hundred points.

"Watch this!" Kurt laughed, and pointed as the top spun back into the middle section and did a double figure eight; knocking down all four brides in a row and sending the last bride hurling into the first section to take out that bride as well. Game over, the six grooms still stood there, alone and looking on with their startled faces.

"You're negative fifty for hitting that last bride." Kurt looked up at the two-way mirror, his laughter still echoing through the game room. "Very funny," said Zella, and turned off the intercom.

She didn't speak to him for the next five days. He apologized over and over for knocking the brides down, but she wouldn't listen. "It was an omen," she told her father. "The wedding is off."

Finally Kurt did the only thing he knew to really get through to her; he bought her a game. Actually it was five games. The French, Russian, Spanish, English, and German versions of the game Sorry. He left them on the doorstep with a note. "I'm sorry," it said. "I'll move four spaces back, but don't knock me out of home base." They were married two days later.

They played more games after they were married, new games. As wedding presents they received Risk and Operation, and from Zella's father a special deck of cards made especially for playing Crazy Eights. Kurt suggested they play games like Doctor and Post Office, but Zella said they were too formless and she preferred a game with more definite rules. Every once in a while they would take out their wedding Skittles game and try to knock each other down, or else gang up on the Minister and send him flying off of the playing field altogether. The painted ring on the spinner had flaked off completely, and after a few years it seemed as if the paint was wearing off of all the pieces.

Kurt started playing in Skittles tournaments every other weekend. He traveled all over the country, and after seven years he was something of a celebrity. He would go to toy store openings and promotions, demonstrating Skittles to children of all ages. Sales reached five million, and often he would be gone as much as six days out of the week. He brought a puzzle of every city he visited home to Zella, and once, after returning from a week long trip he found her on the floor of the game room, surrounded by forty thousand different puzzle pieces. She was trying to fit them together, create one complete picture of his trips. She had mixed a scenic view of the Charles River in Boston, with the Oklahoma City skyline at night. The Golden Gate Bridge ended up on the Mississippi River, and in the center of it all, Old Faithful gushed right up through the Statue of Liberty's head.

"The world," she said, when he walked in, "I created the world."

Kurt put his hand on the top of her head, and ran his

fingers through her hair until they got stuck in the tangles. "I've never been to Yellowstone Park," he said, looking at Old Faithful.

"I know," said Zella, "I ordered that one special."

Kurt came home from a Masters Tournament one weekend, and found Zella sitting silently on their bed, shuffling a deck of cards.

"What's the matter?" he asked, brushing a stray hair off his jacket.

She motioned for him to sit down on the bed. "War," she said and dealt out the entire deck of cards. Actually, it was two decks of cards shuffled together, and they played War for six hours straight. At times he would have only a handful of cards left and she all the rest, but then slowly, round by round, he would start winning her cards back until they were even, and then she only had a handful. It went this way for hours, back and forth, battle by battle, until finally, after a double, triple war hand, he slapped the Ace of Diamonds down and took everything.

"You win."

"What's the matter?" he asked again.

"Nothing." Zella smiled and began separating the decks of cards into two separate piles.

Later that night she came in with another game, Clue. "I'm tired," he said, "No more games."

"One more."

Kurt sat up in their bed. "I have to leave early in the morning. I don't want to play."

Zella set the game up between them on the bed. "A quick game," she said. "It's the least you could do."

She was Miss White and he was Colonel Mustard. He rolled first, a two, and Zella laughed. She rolled a six and headed for the Lounge.

"The Kitchen is closer," Kurt suggested.

"Roll," said Zella.

Kurt rolled a three this time, and Zella laughed again. She rolled another six and landed in the lounge.

"I accuse," she said.

"Suspect or accuse?"

"Both."

Kurt sighed. "You know the rules," he said. "If you suspect you get to go again, but if you accuse, the game is over."

"The game is over," said Zella.

"Accuse then."

"I accuse," began Zella, her voice beginning to waver a little, "Miss Scarlet and Colonel Mustard in the Lounge."

"You can only accuse one person."

"Miss Scarlet, then."

"Okay," said Kurt. "What did she murder with?"

"I'm not accusing her of murder."

"You have to have a weapon!" Kurt yelled. "What is the weapon?"

"The rope."

"The rope?"

"Yes, the rope, the thing you hang yourself with!" Zella grabbed the brown envelope marked confidential, and emptied the cards onto the center of the game. Miss Scarlet, Colonel Mustard, the Lounge and the Rope fell out.

"You cheated."

"I cheated?" Zella threw the game on the floor. "Who cheated?" she screamed, "Who cheated?"

Kurt slumped down in the bed. "I did," he said. "I did, are you happy?"

"No," said Zella.

Kurt retired from the Skittles circuit then, telling the press it was time to move over and let the next generation have a chance. "I'm not getting any younger," he said. "And my family needs me." The papers said the toy community's loss would be felt by all, and speculated about a comeback.

"Never," said Kurt.

A week later he was glad he had retired. A family in Kentucky bought a wedding edition Skittles game at a garage sale, and their child ate one of the pins and almost died of lead poisoning. The press was ruthless, and Kurt knew the bad publicity would have ruined him on the circuit. Proctor and Gamble recalled the games, and Zella's father suffered a fatal heart attack because of it. They buried him five days later.

Zella locked herself in their game room after the funeral, and Kurt, listening at the door, could hear the Skittles pins crashing into each other as the top spun randomly over the game. On the third day, Kurt shoved eight Scrabble letters under the door. The letters spelled, "I Love You." Zella came out and said that was worth forty points, and why didn't they play.

Life settled down after that. Mondays and Fridays were for the old games. Tuesdays were the new electronic memory games, and Wednesdays were video games. Thursdays were for card games: Canasta, War, Crazy Eights, Rummy, and Go Fish. Saturdays were set aside for the formless types of games Kurt liked, and Sundays were for Skittles. Zella never had children because of that very first game of Life, even though Kurt often pleaded with her. "You played that game for marriage," he said, "Not for children."

"I played it for family, and you were the only family the game gave me."

"But it's just a game."

She said nothing.

"It said you would go to the Poor Farm, and that hasn't happened. No fire. No stock market."

"I didn't play for finances. I would've played Monopoly for that."

"We played Monopoly to see where we would live."

"It works for both."

"How about we play Skittles. However many pins we knock down is how many children we have."

"It doesn't work that way," Zella screamed. "There has to be relevance. Those are the rules!"

"We could cheat. Pretend."

"You can't do that." Zella pressed her palms up against her eyes and shook her head back and forth, back and forth. "Those are the rules. Those are the rules."

Kurt put a hand on each side of her face, his palms cupped around her ears, and pressed together gently, then firmer. "Okay," he whispered, "Okay."

Zella broke away from him and backed up. "I thought you knew," she said. "I thought you understood."

And that night he found her in their game room, washing the plastic, colored players of Clue, Life, and Sorry. She polished the silver pieces of the Monopoly game; the iron, the car, the hat, the man on the horse, and then she ironed all the money, starting with the worn and golden five hundred dollar bills. With a cotton swab she cleaned out the grooves of the Scrabble letters, and touched up some scratches on the board. She wiped down twenty-five decks of cards with a special chamois towel, making sure to get both sides and the edges of each card, including the jokers.

When she went over to the Skittles games, he joined her, and together they polished each and every pin and top in their collection. He took out the horizontal and vertical slats of the game, and sandpapered the rough edges, running his finger across to make sure there were no snags. She handed him the wood preserver when he was done, and while he carefully and lovingly ran first a damp and then a dry cloth across the wood, she leaned against the wall, smiled, and watched.

Judith Johnson

Asylum

Judith Johnson is a prize-winning poet, performance artist and fiction writer, former president of the Poetry Society of America, editor of *13th Moon: A Feminist Literary Magazine*, and publisher of *The Little Magazine: A Journal of New Writings*. Her first book of poems, *Uranium Poems*, won the Yale Series of Younger Poets Prize, her most recent, *Cities of Mathematics and Desire*, won the Poetry Society of America's Di Castagnola Prize. She has eight other published collections of poetry and fiction and has been widely published in anthologies and journals, including *The New Yorker*, *Playboy*, *MS*, *Partisan Review* and *The Norton Anthology of Modern Poetry*. She is professor of English and Women's Studies at SUNY Albany, chair of the Women's Studies Program, and the 1995-96 president of the Associated Writing Programs.

Asylum

There are people with skins smooth as mirrors, who, although beautiful, give you nothing of themselves. You put all your will into seeing something human in them, and what you see with such great effort is yourself. I knew a man once who looked like a prophet or an angel. His name was Kenny, his skin mirror-flat. I was living in Brussels, and my housemate picked him up on the road from Ghent and brought him home. His long blond hair hung unevenly down his back, the left much longer than the right by a good four inches. His blond beard trailed down his chest like river water. You couldn't see his eyes through the dusty glasses. Maybe his eye color was grey like a winter lake. Laid back didn't begin to do him justice. He walked with two canes, but sometimes he put them down and walked without them, so I wasn't sure what they were for. No more than twenty-two, he was summering in Europe while avoiding Vietnam, just passing through.

There are people who aren't beautiful, but they're solid, one of a kind, and beyond your ken. You don't forget them, and you can't resist them. I knew a woman once nobody would tangle with. Minette, her name was, or sometimes Mignonne or Minou; her husband called her "Mioue." For a few months she lived next door to me in Brussels. She had one of those flat, pug faces with flared nostrils, as if someone put a hand on her and pushed her face back into the tree it had sprung from. She had short, red hair that stood up in punk points, and broad, flat hands with splayed fingers. She had a flat, gamine figure, but adult-deep, crescent-moon laugh-lines cut into her face. She yelled at her children a lot, sometimes in French, sometimes in slightly accented English. My children played at Minette's house until I stopped them. Sammy and Florrie, the two girls were called, about five and seven years old. Sammy cried but didn't talk. Florrie cried a lot, whined more', talked some. I thought maybe Sammy was deaf, but Minette seemed not to notice. She told me she had been a trained nurse in France before she married an American soldier. She was what you'd call a survivor. She stayed home most of the day, and when she came over to borrow sugar she smelled of sex and Moroccan hash.

The building is something like a castle, something like a factory, something like a warehouse, something like a prison. Square towers hunch over the black stone walls. A locked iron gate cuts through the walls, guarded on one side by a stone gatehouse. About thirty feet out from the building runs a barbed wire fence. Kenny, or some name like that, because we've forgotten his name, can't see the entrance. Maybe it's around back, but he doesn't bother walking around. He pushes his canes between the tendons of barbed wire, spreading them apart, and slips sideways through the gap he has made. The girl is waiting at the gatehouse to let him in.

The girl is very young to wear a nurse's uniform. In fact, it is not hers, she tells him, but her mother's. Her mother is chief nurse in the ward for disturbed women. Her father may be somewhere, but she hasn't seen him since she was little. In another two years, when Minou is old enough, she can work there too, not as chief nurse, not yet, but as a trusted assistant. Ever since she can remember, Minou has played about the grounds of the huge warehouse. It has been her only home. During the war, before it was her home, maybe before she was born, it was a detention center, but then it was liberated. Her homiest memories are not of the bare, unheated, lonely cottage where she used to sleep when her mother had week-ends off, but of this endless, crowded mansion where she has played games her whole life.

When she was very little, before she was old enough to be left at boarding school all week, her mother used to bring her to the asylum and leave her to play in the ward for feeble-minded minors, whose matron promised to look after her. The feeble-minded were not usually dangerous, so it was quite safe to play with them, and very amusing, too, for they didn't often know what they were doing. The matron would tell Minou to clean up this one, to tuck that one's penis back into his pants, to button the girls' and pre-teens' blouses, to pull on their bloomers for them if they had forgotten, and to slap the older boys when they played with themselves. The patients sometimes resented the little girl's attentions. Sometimes she slapped them too roughly, pinched them, or pulled their hair, but a switch from the matron soon brought them to their senses, as much as they could be brought. In recent years, after the matron had assured herself that her colleague's little girl was capable of controlling these patients, and after the patients had become accustomed to the child's authority, the matron sometimes ventured out for a cup of coffee or a glass of wine, leaving Minou in charge.

After a few such experiments, the matron absented herself for longer periods. Minou was now permitted to visit the ward only on weekends and school holidays, but they were frequent enough so that she never lost touch with her patients. She never asked the matron the purpose of these excursions, for she enjoyed her holiday occupation too much to risk losing it. The matron would leave her a peeled willow switch with which to enforce discipline. It amused her to pretend that the ward was a circus, that these weakminded, sometimes lobotomized louts were ponies and lions, and that she was the ringmaster. She flicked her whip and watched them prance in circles, tossing their heads, whinnying when she switched them. She found that a certain twist of the wrist could bring the whip up quickly between their legs, and cause them to rear and leap.

Once she had become assured that the patients would obey her, she first allowed, then encouraged, finally began to force them to expose and handle the hidden parts of their bodies. Some of them were unwilling. They probably remembered that at other times they had been severely disciplined for performing this very act, and sometimes by this very girl.

Nevertheless, she managed to persuade them. She liked to watch their secret faces as they heaved and pulled. Even very young children learned quickly. One day when the matron was longer than usual in returning, a fourteen-year-old idiot, who was scheduled to move to the men's ward as soon as they had a bed for him, held Minou against the wall, pulled the whip out of her hands, and forced his penis into her. It took him a long time to find the way. The others watched him fumble. One or two opened their clothing to get at themselves again. She tells this to Kenny, or whoever, in a light, amused voice. It is one of her attractions, something that will draw him in and make him forget himself for her.

He knows who he is. She can see that he knows. He is not a resident here. For a moment he looked as if he thought that he might be, as if he thought he remembered a place like this, or many places, a house like this, or many houses, endless, square hulks with rows of hooded windows,—were they factories, were they warehouses, were they detention centers that he remembered?— and a girl like this one sitting by his side near a canal, or maybe in a bar or at a café, telling him horror stories in a light, amused voice. Maybe it was this girl, and that was how he met her. Possibly he has memories that do not belong to him, as his hands do not belong to him either, because they move by themselves. He watches his hand touch Minou's crisp, white cap. His voice murmurs, "Come on, let me take this cap off, it will get crushed." He hears Minou laugh, a short throaty laugh, as he takes the cap off, and she shakes out her short, red, spiked, punk hair. They both know who he is, although some time will come when they won't. They know that he has not forgotten himself. They see everything he does. But he is not the one moving this body. Someone else moves this body, someone else twitches its long fingers through the red, spiked cap of the young girl's hair. They watch the stranger whose body he inhabits walk, stiff-legged, with his two canes, into the disturbed women's ward. Minou can see him watching himself. "My mother is out now," she tells him in her lightly accented and amused voice. "She has a sweet cookie man in the men's building, so she leaves me in charge of these cows of hers over here."

"That's why you're wearing her uniform," Kenny guesses.

"Yes, that's why. They're not dangerous, but they won't respect me without it."

"Is respect so important to you?" he asks her, with surprised sincerity, as if he wants to know.

"Respect is everything," she says.

They lie down on a couch in the corner. The disturbed women sit around them, some knitting, some sewing. They cannot be dangerous if they are allowed knitting needles, but they do not look nearly as mild as cows. One rocks back and forth. One croons the Ave Maria repeatedly, but never gets past the first four words. "Won't it bother them?" Kenny asks Minou.

"No," says Minou. "They don't care what we do."

"But won't such sights make them worse?"

"Nothing can make them worse," says Minou, her voice grave and objective. "They don't really understand. In any event, they're used to me. This isn't the first time I've been left in charge here. Actually, this is what you came for, isn't it? There were other girls there, drinking with us. You liked me best. This is what I had to offer."

"What did I have to offer?" he asks her, smiling, as he runs his hand dreamily through her crisp, red spikes. His lips move slowly, experimentally down her throat, pausing over the vein to feel the blood pulse, then crawling onto the shoulder, then onto the breast. He sucks her breast, then raises his head, looks down at the nipple, and blows lightly on it. When it puckers, he touches it with his tongue. He remains, mouth open, tongue slightly out, looking at her nipple.

"Does it really bother you?" she asks.

"What?"

"This. With them watching. I didn't think American men were sentimental."

"I don't know," he says, looking blankly down at her nipple. "It's no big deal, I guess. Most things aren't."

She wonders why he is such a do-nothing. He'd looked vast and quiet and soothing, but not at all out of it, when she picked him up. She'd hoped he would be an adventure. Maybe hospitals bother him. Although he doesn't seem to need his two canes, or even one to walk, he carries them. He must have suffered some injury. Maybe he remembers hospitals, remembers women watching him, nurses tossing him about in his bed, raising him, lowering him, moving his legs for him, holding his penis over the bedpan, wiping his buttocks. Maybe he remembers them holding him under the arms when he relearned walking, holding him over the toilet the first few days he began to use it again. He remembers their cold impersonal eyes observing him as he staggered clumsily up and down the corridors with his aluminum walker, their cold impersonal eyes observing him topple like a child, and wait for one of them to come to his rescue, and their eyes still watching him as he realized that they were not going to help him, that their time for helping him was past, and that now he would have to heave his way to his feet by his own efforts, watched still by their cold impersonal eyes. It was, she suspects, this possibility in him that drew her to him, or this kind of memory in his life that may have drawn him to her. Or, maybe all men have such memories because once they were children. And maybe it was not those qualities he shares with her patients that drew her to him, but the pure, radiant emptiness of his face, even when, as now, he is not smiling. She watches him with cold impersonal eyes as he pulls her panties down. Although maybe he no longer minds the disturbed women watching him, he is still a little sluggish—-not that he cannot rise to the occasion: he can and already has, but he seems not unduly impatient to press things to a conclusion.

Minou doesn't see why he feels no urgency, but she considers herself a reasoning animal. She applies her analytic powers, without success. She stares up past him at the ceiling. She is breathing quickly, but makes no attempt to excite him or to stimulate herself. "They're very quiet," she tells him, in case this is what he needs to know. "They don't even know what we're doing. They don't care. The patients in the dangerous wards care. Some of them know all about it. Some of them like to do all sorts of things. Many of the things they do are truly bizarre. It's risky to monkey around with them. They get excited. But these mooses here, sometimes when things are dull, my mother and I and the other nurses give them things, spanish fly or acid, and we sit here and laugh at the things they do. Some get frightened on acid. They think terrible things will happen to them. When the ones who aren't frightened begin to play with them, or when one of us handles them for her own amusement, they're terrified out of all proportion. They carry on about sin and death and wickedness, about losing their souls, poor lobotomized creatures, as if they thought they still had souls to lose. They think that slugs and serpents and other things are touching their private parts, making them into slaves. They have an idea, of a rudimentary sort, of some great terror waiting for them, but they don't understand that this great terror is sex and their own bodies. Some have had to be moved to the dangerous ward weeks later, when they still had not calmed down. But sex as such is something else. They don't care about it. Even when we give them things to excite them, they don't know what to do. They sit here for a long time, scratching themselves, wriggling their bottoms back and forth on their chairs, grinning or muttering, and we have to take their hands and show them what to do. Then they help each other and laugh, and get all excited, and we laugh like anything. It's only if they were to do it with a man that they'd be scared."

"Are they so funny?" Kenny asks. "Maybe I'd like to see them do those things."

"Why, if it bothers you?"

Kenny thinks a moment. "To know something." He smiles with sudden, astonishing sweetness, although she has no idea what the smile contains.

"We can do that if you like, but first let's finish." She isn't sure whether what he wants to know is about the women or about himself or just about how things are, but whatever it is, she thinks she already knows it and he doesn't.

"Either way, I'm cool about it," Kenny says earnestly, as if he wants to set her mind at rest, as if it matters to do that, as if being cool has the force of a theological or political revelation. "Whatever we do, it's no big deal." He looks at her, then drops his head to her breast again, dispassionately.

Minou throws one arm over his neck and tightens it around him, squeezing hard on the back of his neck with the crook of her elbow. He shoves her legs apart with his knee. A patient has stumbled over one of his canes, where it leans against the wall in a corner. She stands for a moment, muttering, then kneels holding it in one hand while she runs the other quickly up and down it. She takes her lower lip between her teeth and bites down, breathing hard. Humming tunelessly through her nose, she leaps up, hunting and sniffing about the floor at her feet as if she has lost something. Just as she spots the second cane, a small, greyhaired woman like a squirrel snatches it out from under her feet, chittering. The first woman raises her cane also, ready to fight. They stand panting, snarling at each other, hips grinding under the shapeless grey dresses. Minou makes a small, animal murmur. With one accord, both women turn, raise their canes, and begin beating Kenny about the buttocks and shoulders. He screams, in the crisis of his orgasm and helpless. His mind watches some stranger shake his body.

An hour later, half dressed, as he sat sprawled on the couch, Minou spread-eagled loosely across his knees, her hand playing with his scrotum, his hand thrust up to the hilt in her body, they watched the women in the ward fret themselves in the first itch of the aphrodisiac, which Minou had administered with his help. "It's a kindness to them," Minou murmured. "If pleasure is everything, why should they not know something of it too?" The overhead lightbulbs touched the surface of his hair and the air around his head with a golden sheen.

Some time shortly after Minette first moved in next door, my three-year-old came back from playing with Sammy and Florrie, with her wrist swollen and bruised. I asked her how she had hurt herself. She said she had come in the door without knocking. Sammy's Mommy had told her always to knock, then wait to be let in. But how did her wrist get hurt, I asked again. Sammy's Mommy slammed her hand in the door to teach her to knock. I thought about slamming Minette's head in the door for daring to hurt my child, but that wouldn't have guaranteed any child's safety. Even though I immediately forbade my children to play with Sammy and Florrie anywhere but at my house where I could watch over them, sooner or later they'd forget. I waited a few days, then invited Minette over for tea laced with rum. I wanted to soften her before suggesting that I'd be glad to have the children play at my house in the afternoons, and give her some freedom. She told me about her life as a nurse, and about the time she'd had an American who looked sort of like Kenny, the hippy type who had been visiting my house a few weeks before. Her American didn't look exactly like my American. For one thing, the hair wasn't crazy. Her American was a few years ago, before they did that kind of hair. But her American had two canes also, and a laid back outlook, and that was why before Kenny moved on, he had brought to mind her own American piece of marzipan cookie.

"Do you have a thing for Americans?" I asked her.

"American men are candy," she answered. "You can't take care of crazies forever, like my mother. It makes you old too fast."

"Would you have married that other one?" I asked. "The one like Kenny?"

"I was too young then. I was just learning. But yes, why not? Little marzipan ducks first—then potato soup, when you're too old for the sweet stuff." She giggled. "There are no mistakes. He leaves, you leave. I need an American passport, American children, he needs a woman who knows her own way. But he doesn't want to need me long, and I better not need him. Maybe I'll leave Sammy and Florrie with my mother, till they're less trouble. Maybe then we'll go to New York on our American passports. For now, soon, maybe I'll go on the road, maybe move across the borders, carrying some of this good Morocco stuff my husband gets through the NATO trucks. I got a head for business. And Sammy and Florrie, well, my mother taught me, so I guess she can teach them too. 'If you're too stupid to live, you die,' she used to tell me. 'If you stay where they put you, you got no business anywhere. Nobody needs to be stupid in this world.'"

I knew someone once who used to classify people. "That one's a mirror man," or "That one lives by his reptile brain," he used to say. The prophets I've known wanted to show me that my life was all wrong, and the angels couldn't let me change anything about them. Both were what my friend would have called mirror men. But survivors: those are cold and fast-moving. With Minette, you might need to seek asylum. But Minette's mother is the one you should ask to meet, if you're still finding your own way. She must be the mother of all survivors, and she's a mystery. If you look at me, you might see her face, but you wouldn't necessarily know if it was your own or mine, or how to use it.

Carolyn Banks

Random Violence

Carolyn Banks, a regular reviewer for the *Washington Post*, is the author of several suspense novels, a collection of short stories titled *Tart Tales*, and a lighthearted mystery series set in the equestrian world. Her short fiction has appeared in many anthologies, including *Slow Hand* and *I Shudder at Your Touch*. She lives in Texas.

Random Violence

I am squinting at my memory of the days just past, trying to get it clear. The only thing that I'm sure about, though, is this:

I was beaten by another human being, beaten in rage and without reason, beaten by a stranger, a man, someone whose features are foreign to me, out of my reach.

But every thing has its up side, right?

By which I mean that, meanwhile, celebrity—in the form of interviews from my bed piped onto WAKE-UP LINE and GOOD NIGHT AMERICA—has resulted.

"If the person who did this is watching," one of those blonde women asked, "what would you say to him or her?"

"It was a man," I told her. "It was very definitely a man."

"Well, what would you say?" she continued.

I looked straight at the red light. "Thank you," I said, "for stopping when you did."

"Do you think he had you mixed up with somebody?" she asked when we were off the air. "Do you think that's why he stopped?"

"I don't know," I said. "I just don't know."

The next reporter, from another network, was at his investigative best. "Why," he demanded, his eyes narrowing on mine, "have you not consented to hypnosis?"

"Nobody asked me about hypnosis," I told him. "Nobody's mentioned it before."

Or since.

Oh, sure, the police had me look through pictures, had

me sit with someone who flipped a book with interchangeable haircuts and noses and chins, but the fact is, it all happened before I knew it was happening, happened before my senses—even the ones that register pain—knew they would be called into play.

The Rape Crisis Center called me. "I was not raped," I said.

A couple in Lubbock, Texas, invited me to live with them for the rest of my life, room and board free. That scared me more than the beating had. "No, really," I said, not even thanking them.

And then there was an anonymous call asking me if I believed in Karma. Which I do.

After that, I telephoned my mother and asked if I could come to Pittsburgh for a couple of days.

"Why?" she wanted to know.

"Mother, you are probably the only person in America who doesn't know," I said.

"Know what?" She and her husband had been in the Poconos with a square dancing group.

"Never mind," I said, "Never mind."

She told me to take care. My plan exactly.

Anyway, nothing was broken. The x-rays showed that. I was even allowed, right that same day, to go home. My friend Cassie helped me change into an old flannel nightgown and then left me there to sleep, which I did off-and-on for intervals that were punctuated by the ringing of the phone or the doorbell or both. Seven lawyers called and one, a woman, came by the apartment. She had a camera with her and persuaded me to let her take pictures of my naked back.

It was a Polaroid, this camera, because, she said, even in this day and age, they can sometimes give you a hard time about developing pictures like these.

Pictures like these. I kept two of them. It was the only time I had viewed my back injuries, and even I was impressed.

There was no swelling, only a deep purple blood-bloom on my buttock where I'd lain, I guess, on the concrete pavement. "Like a dead person," a nurse had explained, "Not that I want to upset you with that analogy. But that's what happens to the blood, it pools, and that's why you have that bruise." It looks like a birthmark, too big to be hidden by, say, both my hands if I could move my hands to that spot and hold them there.

And then there's my spine. A fist-sized bruise at its base and a progression of black dots running up, up, up, at least as far as my waist.

These bruises are there, still, some twelve days after "the incident."

I didn't let the lawyer photograph my front, where only two marks can be seen, the marks my assailant's hands made when he grabbed me, left shoulder, left groin.

Someone from the local TV station asked me if there were any parallels between my case and the Stewart case in Boston. "What Stewart case in Boston?" I asked. And then he told me, the one where the guy shot his wife dead and then wounded himself and tried to make it look like an attack. And then he jumped in the river when they found him out. "You mean," I said, "did I do this to myself?" And then, even though it hurt someplace in my ribcage, someplace where there wasn't even any mark, I laughed.

Because what happened was this:

He picked me up, this man whose attention was upon me in a way I felt before I saw, picked me up, held me there over his head and then Slam! And I do mean slam. What he did was, he slammed me down against the street.

"Was that all?" the interviewer, the first one, police, tv, I don't know which, had asked.

Yes, that was all. And I lay there for a long while, listening to the sound of cars pulling up and driving off, the sound of soles against the pavement, the way conversations dimmed when they approached me, saw me, just a girl in blue jeans and a sweatshirt and tennis shoes, a girl who was between jobs and living in an apartment complex where they didn't allow kids, a girl who wanted a cat but didn't have one and who couldn't even keep a cactus plant alive. A girl who, at thirty-four, should get used to calling herself a woman, should develop some skills, should get married, maybe, think about having a baby before it's too late.

"What did he look like?" This was someone at the hospital.

"I keep thinking of Anthony Quinn."

"He was Hispanic?"

"I don't know," I said. "Is Anthony Quinn Hispanic?"

Then another voice, a sympathetic voice, "How soon can you get her to x-ray?"

X-ray. "Not my left," I said, "I can't lay on my left."

"It's better on your left," the technician said.

I guess the bruises hadn't come out yet.

"Now exhale all your breath out and hold it, h-o-o-ld it."

"If you'd had to stay at the hospital," Cassie said, "they'd have posted a guard by your room. In case he decided to come back." She said this as she brought me in a tray. All I remember about it was the tang of tomato juice, though there was something solid there, too, something I ate, an Egg McMuffin, maybe. "You probably should try to move," she said, "since nothing's broken."

The terrible things that have happened to me, they have always come this way, boom, no warning.

Like in that aerobics class I was taking, there I was, flat on the floor doing my deep breathing. Then right beside me, a giant splash that barely missed my face, hot tar from the roof, a spill from up there, where men were working.

It landed on my gym bag and it took me seven phone calls, two of them long-distance, before the company would agree to have it replaced.

"Did you see his eyes?" Cassie asked me. "They say that killers don't have any expression in their eyes. That they're flat, you know, like buttons."

I think of a dog who jumped me once when I was a kid. His eyes were like that. But as a matter of fact, there was something about this man's eyes, the man who beat me, a momentary something when my eyes locked on his.

We were level, I remember: his eyes, my eyes, level. Mine were pleading *Oh, don't do this*, and his, his were registering it, I could tell.

"No," I tell Cassie, "There wasn't time."

Today the Center for Random Violence called to ask if I would participate in a study. They would pay me, they said. "It's a heavily funded project," they explained.

"Sure," I said.

I was thinking that when I get there, to the Center, there he'll be, hunched over a clipboard, Anthony Quinn, who'll have done it all as part of an experiment. We'll fall in love, we'll marry, he'll trace the outline of my bruises with his finger, kiss them, maybe, his lips plump against my blood-purpled flesh.

"It's a questionnaire," they say. I'll get it in the mail.

Did I ever live near power lines?

Have I ever seen a UFO?

Did my mother love me?

And my father? My father? What about him?

"You were not beaten," the lawyer, the woman, the one with the Polaroid, is telling me. "Beaten implies repeated blows, blows delivered over a prolonged period of time. So of course yours is a much weaker case."

I wasn't thinking of it as a case. She was thinking of it as a case. It never in a million years occurred to me as a case.

"And the fact that there were no breaks," no shattering of bone.

"Hey," I say, "no problem." I ask about the Polaroids, though.

"Oh," she says, "I don't have them anymore."

Cassie brings me a videotape that she made of one of the initial broadcasts. She and I are staring at a Koppel-like face. "She was beaten," he is saying, and I am behind him, out of focus, bleary-eyed and bleary-faced, propped right, the only way I could, until yesterday, sit.

"Beaten," he goes on, "in rage and without reason, beaten by another human being."

"See," I say.

Then Cassie says, "Did you know there's some kind of fund that the state has for victims? Like, play your cards right and you could make a killing off of this." A minute later, like she's been storing this up, she adds, "Then we could go into business together. Screen tee-shirts or have a video franchise or something. What do you think?"

And this, right here, is where I cried.

Stacey Levine

Scoo Boy

Stacey Levine lives in Seattle. Her collection, *My Horse and Other Stories*, was published by Sun & Moon Press and won the PEN/West Fiction award for 1994.

Scoo Boy

This was my scoo boy, my glider, my street skater, hair long, dark, four tails; he longed someday to be a boxer, a stunt diver, as some boys do. You should have seen him then, my adorable boy born with wings in every gesture of his eye; he was meant to take the money, too, and likewise I was meant to give it to him.

There's no such thing as purity, because that's exclusionary, but this boy shone with the singular uncanny vibration that gives the color copper its peace and glow.

I imagine myself about to give him the money, saying the words, finally: For you.

This takes place just outside the city, where he stayed.

Once I get the money to him, I'm sure to be gratified, exhausted, relieved; I'll sink to my mat, and be able to think once more, about my boy, of course, no other.

He behaves in strange ways I adore, by a code that nobody knows; my gut churns pathetically at the thought of him remaining where he is, in the rankest of places, half-submerged harbors, old city hill crests covered by the ooze of the last century's excesses; I blanch at the thought, pains rise, fasten into constellations in my gut, yet I will be all right if I can just get the money to my boy who desperately needs it.

I would like to be able to get him the money, all at once, straight away; not in installments, just handing it over, my glance forced upward due to the pressure of luminous winds and the flotilla of birds that would have filled the sky then and with a crash disappeared.

I miss him insanely like that, in terrible bursts when night comes in; one evening with the others I sat on the crumbling, dust sodden green, waiting hours for a film to fall into focus on the screen and begin, sadness inhabiting my gut once again when a well-dressed announcer finally emerged and said, "David, the King of Music, has been dead now 16 years to the day," as tears strained down my face, for we believe we have grasped the passage of time until something shocks such belief away; I wore a sticky wreath around my neck in those days, after the boy was first taken, to help express the fondness from my heart, like tears from eyes, so it would not collect or obstruct me or make me blind.

He did nothing wrong, truly, for there is no wrong, only what we already know, and have, and have done. The myths are defunct, you know; the softening of the armies came, and it was far too late; there will be no hope for them, I hope; the building facades have already gone to maroon rust; and many of us disappeared at that time, too; I was told that my father before last seen was running down a cobblestone hill, looking in vain for a transparent button. On another sweltering day, at Soldier's Field, I believe, a begowned, besotted singer wailed to stragglers sitting unsheltered in the sun about the falling down of the world, and a depression the likes of which we had never seen; I stared at my dry, spotted arms, the song burning itself into me; the boy's sweetness was never hidden, I concede, and unless I get him the money somehow with my brittle cunning, duplicitous charm, needle slivers into blisters of want, he will never leave his restraints; still my hopes rise toward the incredible rondure of the blank sky, and, I suppose, to heaven, the place they once decided exists apart and pure and benevolent.

If I can get the money I know the boy will be safe. I know he's waiting, silent each evening; after time this makes him quickly older: that's no good.—Can you imagine where he is, caught up in vaguenesses and steam, some sub- slavering factory-like machine, who can quite know, pulling at straps he doesn't need to pull, one after another in confusion and uncertainty; I have fallen, faltered in my terrible dust covered room imagining this, his bewilderment and sweet striving to maintain some economy of reason and sense throughout; I called him my heartbeat, I remember his up-close scent—

despite the years of twisting, arching heat from the sun beating down and the outrage of dust piled between now and then— an elixir of mercury, the saddest element, full of weight and departure, trails of flint, very thin, and of water, not the water we know now, but as it once was, they say, nearly invisible, yet the most gratifying substance imaginable.

Money will illuminate even the saddest of winters, I say.

If I brought him the money, would it somehow reveal to him my hands, my face?

I have so quietly often wondered what deeds I have done, that might have helped cause them to take him away, my room's chief instrument being the cracked telephone, and who knows murder so deep as speech, they say; on that dry, empty road of apartments, for years dust enthralled, remote, didn't I sit whispering furiously through the line in so many ways, to get things and money done my way?

He did nothing wrong; it's inside the city he waits, not held, nor locked up, yet not at liberty, either—that's the key, the quandry—so that no one can get to him, quite, nor can he leave; I would show him to you the moment he steps clear, reeking gorgeousness, natural plenary elegance of spirit: wouldn't the money accomplish this?—Though money is not real, they say, despite it became so, finally, strengthened by the armies, the canons of power—quite obvious forces steering the way—but wouldn't this money impart exactly what we want, and need?—Buying him free, setting his impeccable feet into the sand—I dreamed all last night of this possibility, of thousands of chaste, awestricken moments beneath the once-living seas, of torrent and rescue and resultant grace; crows, silent helicopters floating to the city's border with goading intent to procure all of this; I remember the grip of his hand; I was older then, now I am young, flying with money and fiendish power to the boy and the center of things, because, after all, power is what we need; I would torture the guardsmen, wring the necks of all cats, smash conveyor belts, bicycles, the histories of our useless lousy kin and their kin before them, to complete this task—the boy is not yet at liberty; who is; the notion of crime does not impress me in the least, nor do the dreams of boys and men, bound to foolish absolutes, the romance of wrongs forgiven in a haze of bliss, or the conviction that the old myths are true—but at the moment of liberty, what will this matter for us, the moment when degradation is no longer part of enjoyment; he and I, and all the rest, escaped within seconds to the tundra or the former capitol of our nation, now overturned in soft clay ruins and vistas, the place where everyone excitedly lives, close to the ground, having buried the words of the dead ones for good; children having untied themselves in a vast and sumptuous explosion of work, words of sooth in their minds as they skatingly move on, and long after we are gone, who knows what they will have uncovered and cleansed from this unmentionable era.

Eileen A. Joy

Lot's Wife

Eileen A. Joy received her MFA from Virginia Common-
wealth University in 1992, and has published fiction and
poetry in *New Virginia Review*, *Short Fiction by Women*,
and *The Sun*. She wrote and co-produced a film, *In Wisconsin, The Blind Can Hunt*, shown at the 1992 International
Gay and Lesbian Film Festival and placing second at the
1992 Chicago Student Film Festival. She is currently working on a Ph.D. in Medieval Literature at the University of
Tennessee.

Lot's Wife

The reports from Sodom and Gomorrah were greatly exaggerated. To say that those two cities were exceedingly wicked is pure flattery. Sodom and Gomorrah were barely cities, let alone exceedingly wicked cities. And to say that Sodom and Gomorrah were two distinct places, even when we understand that a village is of a completely different shape and character than a city, is to stretch the truth beyond its usual limits, unless two collections of mud-baked shacks separated by a few sand dunes has now come to mean "twin cities." Sodom and Gomorrah, though often imagined as two cities rich from the silver wages of sin and populated by contortionists, were, in fact, one place—one small, miserable, completely uninteresting place. Oh, some of the citizens of that place, when traveling, would say they were from Sodom, and some would say, to an inquisitive visitor, this is Gomorrah, but it was all the same thing.

Anyone who had ever been there, when asked to recall their visit, could usually muster only the vaguest of details, the place was so indistinct. If you had ever suffered the misfortune of passing through there, on your way to another place, you might have recalled the gritty taste of the white liquor served in the taverna, how it smelled faintly of anise, or how the women, thick-set and wearing shapeless white shawls, would sit cross-legged in front of their houses, pounding a coarse grain with flat stones and invoking under their breath the name of some terrible god. You might have remembered how this name, repeated again and again, became an ominous chant, the women threading that unspeakable name into a song of lament, a catalog of complaint, or was it a testament to unrequited love?

You might have remembered the heat, how oppressive it was, or how everything was covered with a fine, red dust. The desert never stopped advancing on that place, never stopped shoring itself up in the doorways and on the windowsills, in the cracks of the shutters and in the hollows of your ears. You wouldn't have stayed long. The landscape would have been too forbidding, the people unfriendly. Sodom and Gomorrah was never a destination, or even a place to stop along the way. Who wanted to linger in such a place, not a city or even a town, but just an outpost in the desert, populated by exiles, by people who had only one thing in common: God had forgotten about them.

But even this was not enough to bind them together. Having fled society, the citizens of Sodom and Gomorrah were suspicious of each other and didn't care about fitting in, and this is how we have two names for a village that was barely even a village, because it was necessary to have some kind of border to pass over, a cloak covering your face against the wind, so that you could disparage the one place while sitting in the other, and vice versa. It was necessary to be able to wander over a few dunes and imagine that you had gotten away from a place that was inadequate, where the bread was never crusty enough, and the wine never strong enough, and the women too ugly for consideration, and to have someone listen to these complaints, saying, yes, I don't know how you stand it, but then we have our problems, too.

Perhaps Sodom and Gomorrah had more than one face. Just as it possessed two names, perhaps it also had two natures: Gomorrah for those who passed through unwittingly, a village as pedestrian and morose and forbidding as its name, shutters always closed against the wind, emaciated dogs whimpering outside the taverna's back door, gaunt and sunburnt men passing dented pieces of copper back and forth, never speaking to one another, but always negotiating some piece of business, and the women, as always, invoking that terrible name under their breath while sitting cross-legged on the hard ground. In that place called Gomorrah, no one ever lifts their eyes to the sun or acknowledges a visitor except to take his coins.

And then, perhaps, there was Sodom, a place revealed to only the most discriminating of travelers: dull and humorless Gomorrah by day, illicit Sodom at night, a second, more earthly moon, its name rolling off the tongue like so many other names (sodomy, sodomize, Sodomite), a place where every gesture is perverse, the third door unlocked and no animal too sacred for revelry. In this secret, underground city the women take off their white shawls, revealing their bodies' perfections, and the men, thirsty from the sun, drink red wine from their pale breasts. About this secret city there is much talk in other quarters, though no one will ever confess to actually having been there. It is said that the men, after midnight, turn into wolves and that the women, after lying with them, actually cut out their own hearts to feed them, that they do not die after doing this because they are not really alive to begin with.

But to believe in that place, in that Sodom, is to indulge in a fantasy, for Sodom and Gomorrah. though it was a place with two names, had only one nature. It was always more Gomorrah than it was Sodom. Everyone who lived there knew what was said about them, and occasionally someone would say to a traveler, "I'm from Gomorrah, I know nothing of Sodom," as if that would save them. But God had already decided, had already left his footsteps behind in the dunes' shallow indentations, the red sand always shifting with the wind, erasing his tracks.

Each morning in this village, Lot's wife would take her broom and sweep the desert away from her door. This was the only time when Lot, still sleeping, could not bother her with his prophecies. He often heard voices, which he didn't keep to himself. He was convinced that God spoke to him, that God had special messages only for him. In a village starved for entertainment, he played the fool. Lot's wife suffered for it. She was shunned at the well by the other women, and if she refused to take Lot's word on any matter, words ordained by God's small and furtive voice, she was beaten for her disrespect, beaten with the same broom she wielded against the desert.

If we could give Lot's wife a name, if we could call her Sarah or Rebecca or Ruth or Jessica, Leah or Delilah or Naomi or Kezia, we could perhaps imagine her more vividly, but it is not possible to name her now, any more than it would be possible to finger a strand of her coarse, black hair, or to watch her slim shoulders bent over the well as she pours water into two leather skins, or to taste her posole, served with oatcakes and mulled wine, to taste her labors in the coarse grain pounded into sweetness. If a woman in these times was beloved by a son, she was named. But Lot's wife had no sons. She had two daughters—two surly, oily-haired daughters who no more cared to love her than to name her.

These daughters disdained all household chores, spending most of their time with their father, whom they worshipped, believing everything he told them about God and angels. They wouldn't help their mother tend to the goats or hang the linens out to dry, preferring instead to accompany Lot as he made his rounds each morning, going from house to house, the same houses every day, warning everyone of God's displeasure. Occasionally someone would say, "what have we done?" and Lot would just shake his head. To be privy to the word of God was to be privy to so many terrible secrets. In the afternoon, Lot would take his two daughters to the gateway of the village where they would kneel on the dunes, facing east, and pray to God to give them the strength to live in such a heathen place.

At dusk, Lot and his two daughters would return and sit at the table, waiting to be served, never thanking Lot's wife who would spend each afternoon preparing their meal, eating her own portion in silence after her husband had gone to bed. The two daughters would often stay up late, sitting by the fire and smoking artemesia out of a narrow sandstone pipe, exchanging stories about the wicked villagers who were not really wicked, and letting the languor of the mugwort herb wind slowly move through their veins. Though Lot's wife was disappointed with her daughters, and though they never helped her with the evening chores, leaving the table each evening after fits of belching, she did not chastise them.

When Lot's wife went to join her husband in bed, after feeding the goats and pounding the grain in preparation for the morning meal, after putting out the fire and throwing the red cinders outside, the two daughters were usually on either side of their father, white shifts covering their sallow, uncaressed skin, their arms thrown over his bare, narrow back in a protective embrace. Even though there was room for everyone on the thin mattress, Lot's wife would sleep on the floor at the foot of the bed.

On some nights, Lot's wife would leave her body. While everyone in the village was asleep, except for a few men standing outside the taverna, kicking red stones back and forth with their sunburnt feet, she would float above the two towns like a dark angel. She would linger above the rooftops, noticing the uneven weave of the straw, the hens nesting in their coops. Sometimes she would leave Sodom and Gomorrah and fly over the dunes to the mountains. By the edge of a stream there she would sometimes weep, not wanting to return to her body, but it was inevitable.

One day, before dawn, two men dressed in sheepskins came to the door of Lot's house. They had traveled for two weeks on horseback and they were anxious to see Lot. Lot's wife invited them in, but they insisted on remaining outside the house. There was no time, they explained, for visiting. They had come a long way, and they wanted to return as soon as possible. Lot's wife roused her husband from his sleep and he went outside unclothed, he was so urgently needed. The men explained to Lot that they had been sent by Abraham, a distant cousin of Lot's. They explained that Abraham was going to be bringing troops to Sodom and Gomorrah within the month with the intention of burning the two villages to the ground, a political necessity, but Lot was going to be spared. After all, he was a relative of the king's.

All Lot had to do was pack his belongings and move to the mountains, along with his wife and his two daughters. After things calmed down, they could move on. Abraham was a ruthless warrior, but he had a soft spot for family. When you are making your way to the mountains, they told him, do not look back at your village, for the smoke from the fire will blind you. Lot asked the two men if they would come in to his house. My two daughters are virgins, he told them, and you can do what you like with them; spend the night here, and wash your feet.

We cannot stay here, they told him, Abraham is waiting for us. When the two men left, their horses kicked up storm of red dust which made Lot's eyes fill with tears.

When Lot went back to his bed, he told his wife and his two daughters that he had been visited by two angels, and that God was coming soon to destroy their wicked village. Lot's wife groaned and got up to prepare their breakfast, but the two daughters wanted to hear more of what the angels had said. Lot told them that God was displeased with the villagers and wanted to punish them. God was angry, so angry he was going to destroy the two villages with fire. Lot's two daughters became very excited—they had never seen a village destroyed by God before. An erotic charge coursed through their limbs.

"I'm afraid you will be disappointed," Lot told them, "for the angels have instructed me to take my family to the mountains before God arrives, and it would not be possible to watch without going blind. We alone have been spared from His wrath."

Lot's two daughters were sad that they weren't going to be able to witness the destruction of the two villages, but they had never seen the mountains before, having been surrounded their entire lives by the flat, red desert, and they wanted to know when they would be leaving.

"In a few days," Lot told them. "I will tell you when."

But Lot was not too anxious to leave Sodom and Gomorrah. Though God had spoken to him many times, Lot had never actually seen Him and he was hoping to see, if even out of the corner of his eye, God's grim expression. Every day, when his daughters would ask him if they were leaving soon, Lot would tell them, "tomorrow, we will leave tomorrow." But when the next day arrived, Lot would say the same thing. "We will leave tomorrow," he would say.

As the weeks went by, the two daughters grew impatient, moving their thick legs under the table in motions of restlessness each night at dinner. Lot's wife was more concerned about the two men who had visited the house that one morning than she was about her daughters' and husband's eagerness to run after angels. The two men were real. She had seen them in their sheepskins, and they had come in on horses. Only men from

Abraham's court had horses. She didn't know what to think, and Lot had not confided in her.

After a month had passed and Abraham's troops had still not arrived, Lot began to worry, but he needn't have worried. Great warriors rarely show up on time. The distance from Abraham's court was long, and Abraham had stopped along the way to stage some unplanned assaults, and rape a few wayward milkmaids. Abraham was famous for being impulsive. His heart was impetuous.

One morning, about two months after the angels had visited Lot's house, Lot was awakened in his bed by a distant rumbling, like the sound of thunder, only there was never any thunder in that part of the country. He roused his two daughters and his wife from their sleep and told them that he could hear God walking through the sky, that God was going to keep his promise. Lot's wife was alarmed because she could hear the thunder, and her cupboard was rattling, her goats' teeth chattering in reply.

Lot told his wife and two daughters to get dressed, that the time had come for them to leave. Lot's wife ran outside to see with her own eyes what was approaching, because even though she knew she was leaving, she wanted to know what it was she was running from. On the edge of the yellow horizon, she saw a mass of black figures, crooked sticks, which seemed to be rising up out of the ground, one after the other. As they came closer, she saw that the black figures were men on horseback, hundreds of men, all carrying torches and galloping furiously towards their village.

Lot's wife had never packed anything because she had never believed Lot's story, but now she could see that he had known something all along about the fate of the village. She could only guess that he now felt his prophecies as vindicated, and the people of Sodom and Gomorrah as too wicked to be saved. But of wickedness, the people of Sodom and Gomorrah had tasted nothing, they were so deprived. As for Abraham, he wanted everything, even the lousy desert.

When Lot's wife finally went back inside and began to fill a sack with clothing, she did so out of fear. She did not want to die by fire—better to starve in the mountains than to die by

Abraham's torch. Though she was weary of her life, she was not ready to have it end so suddenly. As she was tying kindling sticks into a bundle, her daughters were combing Lot's hair and beard, brown sacks tied around their wide, ample waists. They rubbed oil on Lot's face and neck, their thick fingers kneading his parched skin, so that the wind would not chafe him.

When they were a few hundred yards from the village, Lot walking briskly, only a stick in his hand, his daughters carrying his belongings slung over their backs, his wife carrying the bread and skins of water while dragging the one chosen goat on a piece of rope, Lot's wife remembered something she had left behind. She had forgotten her broom. Surely, even in the mountains, a broom was necessary. There was always some piece of the world which had to be kept back, swept away, held from the hearth. Though this broom had left its marks, had bruised her shoulders and thighs, she was afraid she would lose strength without it, the only thing she had ever held on to with both hands. And though Lot told her that she would be foolish to turn back, that God was already upon the village, that the smoke would blind her, she turned back.

It has been said by some that when Lot's wife turned back towards Sodom and Gomorrah, she was turned into a pillar of salt, proving Lot's warning. Why salt? Because it is sharp and bitter on the tongue, the spice of recrimination? Lot's wife got as far as the back of her house when some of the other villagers, fleeing their burning huts, noticed her and shouted out, "there is the woman who is the cause of our misery!" At that very same moment, one of Abraham's men rode over her, trampling her with his horse. Her skull was crushed, the imprint of her face pushed, roughly, into the red sand. When Lot turned to see if his wife might be returning to join them, he only saw thick smoke rising from the earth like the smoke of a lime-kiln.

Lot and his two daughters made it to the mountains after several months of difficult traveling. At one point, wolves attacked them and ate their goat. They found a cave in which they could dwell together and decided to wait for God's next command. Several years passed. They subsisted on roots and berries. One winter, when it was so cold that icicles were hanging over their bed, the two daughters awoke one night and contemplated their sleeping father.

"He is old," one of them said, "and will not live much longer."

"Suitors will never find us up here," the other one agreed, because they were both thinking the same thing. "Let's make our father drink wine and then lie with him and in this way keep the family alive through our father."

That night, the two daughters took their pleasure with their father after giving him wine, and he was so drunk, he did not know when the first daughter lay down and when she got up. And it was the same with the second daughter. And they did this on many other nights as well. In this way, they passed the long winter, fucking all of Christendom into being.